D0188964

FOR ALL THE GOLD
IN THE WORLD

Massimo Carlotto

FOR ALL THE GOLD IN THE WORLD

*Translated from the Italian
by Antony Shugaar*

Europa
editions

Europa Editions
214 West 29th Street
New York, N.Y. 10001
www.europaeditions.com
info@europaeditions.com

Translation by Antony Shugaar
Original title: *Per tutto l'oro del mondo*
Translation copyright © 2016 by Europa Editions

Library of Congress Cataloging in Publication Data is available
ISBN 978-1-60945-336-7

Carlotto, Massimo
For All the Gold in the World

Book design by Emanuele Ragnisco
www.mekkanografici.com

Cover illustration by Emanuele Ragnisco

Prepress by Grafica Punto Print – Rome

Printed in the USA

I look at the moon,
I look at the stars,
I see Cain and he's smoking cigars.
I see the table set for a meal,
I see Cain frying the veal.
I see St. Peter with a bottle of wine,
And he and Cain are playing at nines.
(NURSERY RHYME)

CONTENTS

FOR ALL THE GOLD
IN THE WORLD

PROLOGUE

J azz woman. When she pressed her red lips to the microphone to sing *Good Morning Kiss,* I'd hold my breath so I could savor every single moment. She was imitating Carmen Lundy's voice and style, but you had to strain to notice it. She'd never make it big, not even in the small-town clubs. She sang jazz songs because they were the one thing that kept her clinging to a life she could barely stand.

Her husband was certain she had a lover. He'd given me five hundred euros fresh from the ATM to find out the man's name. The husband was a good man, still in love, no plans to divorce. All he wanted was to understand why the love of his life had pulled away from him, from their life, for some other man. Some stranger, most likely.

An apparently simple case for an unlicensed private investigator who, for a moderate fee, was happy to stick his nose into married couples' personal business, where it really didn't belong, and who forgot everything he'd found out the minute he was paid.

A couple days was all I'd needed to find out the woman was pretending to go to the hospital, where she worked as a nurse, for a nonexistent night shift, and was actually slipping into a basement spot known as Pico's Club. She'd put on a short, emerald-green dress with a low neckline and a matching pair of shoes, very high-heeled, and she'd get lost in her jazz. She was a generous singer and she gave the songs her all. I knew the piano player who backed her up by sight; he was good but always short on cash so he'd take any gig he was offered. He told me that "Cora" had just showed up one day and asked him for an audition. They performed two nights a week, but she refused to consider taking on any more bookings.

The musician had decided that the woman thought a little too much of herself and had no intention of following his sage advice. A judgment both harsh and uncalled for. She needed to play the star in a hideaway where, for a few hours, reality couldn't get at her. I could have wrapped the case up then and there. But that's not what I did. I violated my bond of trust with my client. I had no intention of cheating him out of his retainer, but it had been two months, and I still hadn't been able to tear myself away from the jazz woman. I'd fallen in love. I liked her. I wanted to be her lover. But I didn't know how to approach her. I certainly couldn't admit that I'd been tailing her on her husband's behalf, and that I knew all about her double life. I didn't want to scare her, much less piss her off. I wanted to love her.

When she was onstage, she sometimes fiddled with the hem of her skirt, and I dreamed of reaching up and stroking her thighs. They were nice, shapely thighs. Cora was in her mid-forties, tall and slender, and her body testified to the effects of a dedicated workout regime—her tits especially. A cascade of curly black hair framed a delicate-featured oval face.

In order to avoid crossing paths with her spouse, who left home to head for work, she'd stop in a café on the outskirts of town for a breakfast she ate slowly. I'd sit nearby and peek at her, admiring the creases at the sides of that mouth I so yearned to kiss.

When I spied on her in the dark at Pico's Club, where she wore that heavy makeup that stood out under the honey-yellow stage lights, she was Cora. Once she changed out of her stage clothes, she went back to being Marilena. Marilena Dal Corso.

That morning, too, I watched her as she bit hungrily into a croissant and read the paper. Suddenly she glanced up and looked me straight in the eye. I smiled at her. She remained expressionless. For a second I was afraid she'd recognized me and connected me to the club. Instead, she went back to her breakfast and paid me no further mind.

I followed her to where she lived, an apartment building on the outskirts of the city. It was practically the countryside. Padua was several miles away. I got out of my car and smoked a cigarette, fantasizing about ringing the doorbell and slipping into the shower with her.

There'd been other times in my life when the desire for a woman's love had literally overwhelmed me, but I was finding this especially hard to handle. I felt an urgent need for her because I was struggling to hold a past filled with old wounds, wounds that had never completely healed, at bay; a past that threatened, every day, to invade. And destroy.

I had no intention of coming to terms with those old skeletons; I knew I'd only emerge a beaten man. I wanted to live in a dignified present. Nothing but love or the stress of a dangerous investigation could guarantee me that. But I wasn't planning to get myself in trouble. I wanted to give and receive tenderness and affection. Kisses and caresses.

I got back in my car and drove to the big-box home appliance store where her husband worked. I waited for him to finish with a customer who wanted to know all about the latest dishwasher models; then I told him that Marilena wasn't cheating on him and gave him back his retainer.

At first he pretended to refuse the money but I cut him off, reminding him of his monthly salary.

"But I'm sure there's another man, she's lying to me, inventing shifts at the hospital," the man said; he was working himself up, his voice growing slightly louder.

I laid my hand on his chest to reassure him. "Your wife is a singer," I told him. "In a shitty club, a place filled with solitary drinkers and older women whose voices are hoarse from too many cigarettes. It's her island of freedom, her harmless little secret. If you take even that away from her, you'll lose her for good."

"I don't understand," he stammered.

"We're men, and there are things beyond our capacity for comprehension. Take my advice: Let her live in peace."

I shook his hand and left the store feeling relieved. The case was solved. Maybe I'd manage to keep my distance from her, as common sense demanded. Maybe. My outlaw heart had other thoughts on the matter.

I rummaged through the CDs I kept in the car and immediately found the one with the piece I wanted to hear: *Dengue Woman Blues* by the great Jimmie Vaughan, brother of the late, lamented Stevie Ray.

I had a hard time finding a parking place near my home and I spent a good fifteen minutes creeping along at walking speed, hunting the adjoining streets for a spot. Then I stopped in at my usual café-tobacconist to stock up on cigarettes. Sometimes I used the place as my general delivery. If someone wanted to get a message to me, they could just leave it there.

Some guy who'd been feeding euro after euro into one of the slot machines lined up across from the bar left his stool and came over. I knew him well. In Padua's organized crime circles he was known as the Bulldozer because his specialty was stealing heavy machinery and fencing it in Eastern Europe.

"Siro Ballan wants to see you," he said softly. "Tonight, if possible. What should I tell him?"

"That I'll pay a call."

He nodded, satisfied. "I'll let him know."

"Can I get you something?" I asked. It was a formality; I was hoping he'd say no.

He pointed at the slot machine that was sucking money out of his pockets like a vacuum cleaner. "I can't leave this thing," he explained. "I have to punish it."

In the elevator I ran into the tenant who lived on the floor below me, Signorina Suello, an energetic seventy-year-old. "I sleep lightly and you always play the music too loud," she complained resignedly.

"Marijuana," I whispered. "Smoke some before going to bed and the blues will sound like a lullaby."

She laughed, flattered by my audacious provocation. It was a little skit we'd been doing for a while now. "Tonight I'm making eggplant parmesan," she announced, "which I know your friend Max really likes. If I happen to make a little too much . . ."

"I sure hope you do."

Max the Memory was my partner. And a true friend. We shared a large apartment with plenty of light, tastefully furnished, in the center of Padua. It had been a gift from a Swiss client who had more money than she knew what to do with. She'd bought the a place as a hideout: There she could have, in blessed peace, a happy and extremely secret love affair with a man who wasn't the husband who paid for her upkeep. A cruel and perverse criminal had tried to exploit the situation to his own advantage, demanding a sizable sum in exchange for not revealing her illicit tryst. The whole story had ended in the worst possible way and the woman had gotten rid of her love nest with a gesture both elegant and generous.

This morning, like every morning, Max was reading the papers in search of information for his archive. He'd started doing it in the seventies and had never given up keeping tabs on local criminals and notables. Information that he'd always processed with remarkable acumen.

Not too long ago, he'd taken a bullet to his flab in order to protect me. The doctors had discovered that his cardiac and metabolic conditions weren't exactly topflight and had ordered him to avoid excess. Food and alcohol only as pre-scribed. He was forbidden to smoke. And so, in fact, Max now only smoked my cigarettes.

"This evening you've got a pan of eggplant parmesan coming to you," I announced as I handed him my pack and my lighter.

He shook his shaggy head decisively. "Not a chance," he retorted. "I have an appointment in one hour with a nutrition-ist. I'm changing my life, Marco."

I sighed. This was the umpteenth specialist since he'd been released from the hospital. I'd lost count. "And how did you find this one?"

"At a pastry shop. I happened to be eavesdropping on a conversation between two women and finally I asked for more information."

Of course, at a pastry shop. "You know how it's going to end, don't you?"

He fell silent, pretended to focus on his reading. Then he burst out, "It isn't easy to find the right doctor, who can help you achieve appreciable results."

"Which, translated into actual weight, means forty-five pounds," I specified in a flat voice. "You need to check your-self into a clinic for rich people where, between a massage and a sauna, they'll offer you salads, smoothies, and transparent slices of pineapple. And, when you fall off the wagon, they punish you elegantly."

He didn't dignify my observations with a reply. He tapped another cigarette out of my pack and smoked it, nervously.

I told him about the jazz woman and the conversation I'd had with her husband. He threw his arms wide, feigning exas-peration. "You fire judgments about my diet decisions left and right, and then you behave like a schoolboy."

"I returned the retainer. I have no further fiduciary respon-sibilities toward that client," I clarified before changing the subject. "Any news about old Rossini?"

"He went to Monfalcone to take delivery of his new speed-boat. Can you guess what he's decided to call it?"

"Sylvie," I replied confidently. The woman he'd loved more than anyone else in his life, the woman who'd never quite been able to recover from the torture she'd suffered during a long kidnapping. She'd killed herself before our eyes. I couldn't help thinking about it every damn day. I understood her decision and I'd been glad that she'd chosen to share it with us, her friends. What I couldn't stand was the fact that we'd rescued her too late, after the worst had already happened. Her captors had paid with their lives, but sometimes that wasn't enough to hold the melancholy of her absence at bay.

Beniamino was a bandit. A smuggler and a thief. That's what he'd always been. We'd met him in prison, and he hadn't been like the others. The criminal world was populated by people devoid of human qualities. His human qualities, in contrast, were extraordinary. As we took turns watching each other's backs, we became friends and decided to face our destinies together, as a team.

Max got ready for his appointment. He wore a light-colored jacket over his navy-blue shirt and his jeans. On his feet were a pair of brown loafers. They'd come back into fashion.

He said that May was striding determinedly toward June, and that it was hot out this morning. Maybe that afternoon the temperature would drop; it often rained later in the day, and thunderstorms cooled the air.

"You're stalling," I said, teasing him. "You're probably going to be late."

He left, slamming the door behind him. I read the local papers. The upcoming regional elections were being fought out over issues like immigration, the Roma, and crime. Mayors were having themselves photographed with reassuring rifles in their hands. The Veneto would vote with its gut; that's how it'd choose the winner.

In Padua, a group of young people had organized a giant drink-in in Prato della Valle; they called this Woodstock of alcohol the Botellón. For the past few years, they'd been getting their kicks by drinking like idiots one night a year. They already did it every day in the piazzas of the city, guzzling down dozens of gallons of spritz, but the minute it was an organized event, the city declared it illegal. The mayor had closed the area off with metal fencing, police patrols, and a myriad of ordinances, threatening to report to the postal police anyone who dared to share news of the event on Facebook. A genuine leader of the community.

City hall was perpetually at war with someone. A charitable woman had taken in a number of Nigerians who had fled from areas controlled by Boko Haram jihadists and survived the trip across the Mediterranean to the island of Lampedusa; for this she had been harshly criticized by the city's first citizen. An association of Paduan shopkeepers had protested by organizing a torchlight parade meant to ward off a potential outbreak of human kindness and solidarity. Among those marching, there may well have been merchants who were laundering money for the Mafia, which suddenly seemed less dangerous when its rivers of dirty cash helped to prop up the economy in a time of crisis.

Nothing too surprising. Northeast Italy is a complicated territory, split between mountains and plains. And swamps that aren't marked on the maps. Swamps everywhere. Full of dangerous, lethal snakes. Places where an alligator could wallow, rake the muck, make some trouble.

I went to honor to the ritual of the aperitif in Piazza delle Erbe. I took a seat in the sunlight, showing off a pair of vintage sunglasses with extremely dark lenses. I'd paid perhaps more than I should have for them in a shop that specialized in mid-century modern accessories.

I called my friend, the saxophonist Maurizio Camardi, and

asked him what he knew about "Cora." He knew everyone in the jazz world.

"She studied singing at my school but I haven't seen her for a while."

"She's performing at Pico's."

"I think that's about the best she can aspire to," he commented. "But you didn't call me about her vocal skills."

"I like her but I don't know how to approach her."

Maurizio was known as an expert on beautiful women and matters of the heart. "I don't know her well, but I've always had the impression that for her, jazz is some kind of escape or therapy."

"That's exactly right."

"Then get interested in her music," he recommended. "That's the only place where you can meet her on common ground."

I ordered a glass of white wine, wondering, frankly, just how attractive I might be to a woman like her.

Max the Memory showed up a few minutes later, interrupting my train of thought. He was furious. Along with the spritz, he ordered a panino with garlic salami and pickled vegetables.

"That woman's out of her mind," was the preamble to his usual rant. "And she isn't even as thin as you'd expect from someone who chisels a hundred fifty euros out of you just for saying that a diet is sacrifice, and that if you want to lose weight you have to give up everything, and that it takes a stiff upper lip. And while she's unloading this mountain of bullshit, she's waving a bag of julienned fennel and carrots under my nose. She comes talking to *me* about sacrifice? And with that arrogant tone of voice? My life is so riddled with holes that if I wanted to fill them all up I'd have to eat a continent."

Max had turned purple. He practically grabbed the panino out of the waitress's hand and chomped into it voraciously.

The last time he'd had dealings with a weight-loss professional he'd vanished for three days; I'd finally tracked him down in an *agriturismo* in the countryside around Parma where they made a first-rate *gras pist*—pork lard, pounded and flavored—which he was a complete sucker for.

For Max, too, the problem was the past. Shattered dreams, on the run from the law, then jail, his woman murdered by gangsters. Stories you couldn't tell on a psychoanalyst's couch.

The fragility of existence haunted him. He was paying the price, just as yours truly and Rossini were, for living in a world made to measure, in a niche halfway between a world of crime that horrified us and a decadent country that had no intention of changing.

"I'm done with this crap," he grumbled through a mouthful of food. "It'll go however it goes. I don't have the energy to pretend I'm a civilian."

We smoked a couple of cigarettes in silence, watching the people crowded around the fruit and vegetable stands.

"Tonight I'm going to pay a call on Siro Ballan," I said suddenly.

Max stared at me, chewing the news over. Then a beautiful woman walked by; distracted by her ass, he went back to watching the passersby.

PART ONE

S iro Ballan wasn't much good as a luthier. Actually, he wasn't much good as a human being either. He was as mediocre as his instruments. He was a tall, skinny man, resentful and unpleasant, who lived all alone in a big house in the country that had belonged to his family for generations. He turned the old granary into a workshop, which smelled of essential oils, shellac, and all sorts of wood: Norway spruce, cherrywood, maple, ebony, rosewood, and boxwood. Along the walls, in no particular order, were a number of tables on which were scattered pieces of soundboxes, as well as necks that went with violins, mandolas, and double basses, all covered with a light layer of dust.

Siro Ballan didn't live off the money he earned from musicians. Over time, he'd built a reputation in the field, but that wasn't what he'd been aspiring to when he'd stubbornly sat down to learn a profession for which he clearly had no gift whatsoever.

If he could afford a certain kind of life, it was due to his large house, which he rented out by the hour. If a gang of bank robbers needed a quiet little place to wait for the police to tire of chasing them, then the luthier would offer them his stables, where it was possible to hide automobiles and delivery vans.

Generally speaking, the most asked-after spot in the house was the living room, reserved for encounters between people looking for a meeting place both absolutely confidential and on neutral ground.

I awaited my potential new client while sipping a grappa cut with Elixir di China, comfortably seated in one of the light-brown velvet-upholstered armchairs, the only lighter note in a room dominated by dark wood furniture.

I heard the sound of a car braking on the pea gravel, followed by that of three car doors slamming.

"That's a lot of people," I thought to myself, my curiosity piqued.

When I found myself face-to-face with the three guys, I realized that this was a gang or, at the very least, a delegation made up of a gang's most important members. The boss was the first one to introduce himself. "Nicola Spezzafumo," he said, extending his hand.

In the underworld he was known as Nick the Goldsmith because he specialized in heists and burglaries from jewelery stores and jewelers' workshops. I knew that he'd taken several years in prison like a man, a mark of his character that made him worthy of respect in my eyes.

He must have recently turned fifty and he'd put on a jacket and tie to come to this meeting. The other two were younger. Not much over thirty. Giacomo and Denis. Elaborate hairstyles from a small-town barber, tattoos on their necks and the backs of their hands.

A round of hard liquor and cigarettes to give the new arrivals a chance to size me up properly. The case had to be a sensitive one. I considered their indecision rather offensive, but curiosity kept me in my seat. After an exchange of glances, Spezzafumo made up his mind to speak.

"On November 27th, two years ago, three armed, masked men broke into a country villa outside of Piove di Sacco immediately after dinner, murdering the owner of the house and his housekeeper. His wife and daughter survived because they'd just left to attend a dance recital at the parish church."

I nodded. I remembered the case. It had been on the front

pages of the local papers for months because of the savagery of the murders. This kind of thing had happened before. The intruders knew that there was a safe in the place and they needed the combination to get it open. The victims were uncooperative, and that then unleashed a burst of senseless violence.

The housekeeper, a woman in her early forties originally from Pordenone, had taken the brunt just because she was a woman. The bastards had had their fun with and then pitilessly tortured her until the gunshot to the head came as a genuine act of mercy, putting an end to the poor woman's suffering.

Then it had been the man's turn. A businessman, forty-seven, he and his wife had set up a small atelier to produce cashmere garments. He'd refused to talk as long as he could simply because he knew they'd never leave him alive anyway. The autopsy had revealed the presence of deep burns over much of his body and a bullet hole in his skull.

The subsequent investigation, though meticulous, hadn't produced any definitive results, as the detectives like to say at press conferences when they've come up empty-handed. An anonymous letter, probably written by a neighbor, had reported the presence of three men dressed in black, their faces concealed by ski masks, seen leaving the house dragging three wheeled suitcases. After a short distance, they'd vanished down a country lane where they'd most likely concealed their car.

"I don't understand what this has to do with your business," I said. "Was the owner of the villa a friend of yours?"

"His name was Gastone Oddo and he was one of us," Nick the Goldsmith replied, watching for my reaction. I didn't bat an eye, and he decided to go on. "He hid our 'merchandise' and our weapons, laundered our money, and invested our profits for us."

I glanced at his confederates. Denis's eyes were glistening. The other man lit a cigarette, his head hunched low. The late Gastone had been well liked.

"Rivals?" I asked.

The three of them shook their heads. "We've investigated, looked into all the crews," Spezzafumo explained, "both Italian and foreign. We've kept a close eye on all the fences from here to Belgrade. Whoever those butchers were, they aren't in our line of work."

"So what's your theory?"

The boss let his men answer that question. "A one-off gang," Giacomo replied.

Denis put out his cigarette. "Someone put it together for this one hit and then dissolved it."

"How much was the take?" I asked.

"About two million between the gold, the precious stones, and the cash," Spezzafumo replied. "We'd just pulled off a job," he hastened to explain, seeing my astonished expression.

"Did they take the weapons with them?"

"Three Kalashnikovs, handguns, ammunition. They didn't leave anything behind."

"Maybe they just didn't want the police to find them," I commented. "They were careful to cover up any clues that would point to the robbery's true objective."

I thought the situation over for a couple of minutes while the three men whispered among themselves, shooting me glances the whole time. Their distrust was palpable.

"The robbers knew that Oddo was your treasurer," I said in a clear, confident voice. "And they knew that that night they'd find the loot from your latest robbery in the safe. Now, I wouldn't dream of offending you, but it seems clear to me that whoever screwed you knew your business all too well."

"That's what we thought from the minute it happened," Denis shot back, some heat in his voice, "but it wasn't any of our guys. We went over all of Gastone's contacts with a fine-toothed comb. We didn't miss a thing."

"What about his wife?" I asked, just to rule that out.

Spezzafumo waved his hand in the air irritably. "She loved Gastone; she never would have betrayed him."

"The housekeeper?"

Denis shrugged. "She was half an idiot, and she didn't know a thing anyway."

Nick the Goldsmith pulled an envelope out of his jacket and tossed it onto the coffee table, cluttered with glasses and ashtrays. "These are the last thirty thousand euros. If you get the loot back for us, we'll give you ten percent."

A nice pile of cash that would come in handy. "How would the rest be split?"

"Half to us and half to Gigliola, Gastone's widow."

I blew out my cheeks. "I'm not taking the case."

"What the fuck are you saying?" Giacomo blurted out, jumping to his feet. "You should have made that clear before you let us tell you all our fucking private business."

His boss put a hand on his shoulder and made him sit back down. "Why not?" Spezzafumo asked.

I poured myself another glass of liquor. "If I were to track down the culprits you'd do everything within your power to make them pay, and I don't want to risk spending the rest of my life in prison thanks to a vendetta that has nothing to do with me. These stories always end badly. Funerals, cops, and the smart guy who sells the others down the river before they get a chance to do the same to him."

Denis clenched his fists and Giacomo glared at me. Nicola, on the other hand, spoke carefully. "Our operations would be secure, you know that's how we work: It's no accident no one's ever caught us."

I shrugged my shoulders. "That's no guarantee and anyway, there's another aspect to this story that I don't like . . . "

Denis interrupted me and turned to Nick the Goldsmith. "Afterwards, do me a favor and explain why the fuck you insisted on bringing this asshole into it in the first place."

I ignored the insult and went on explaining my reasoning. "If you get the money, by rights it ought to be split three ways. The housekeeper was an innocent victim, she had nothing to do with your work; she was in that house working for a salary and she was tortured to death."

Denis and Giacomo snickered. Their chief shook his head. "If you don't mind, that's our business."

"Exactly," I agreed as I stood up.

Nick the Goldsmith shook my hand. He knew his manners. The other two glared at me menacingly. They were too young to know that the roads criminals tread are paved with stupid hotheads.

I left them to Siro Ballan and his idle chitchat. He always livened up the moment of payment with a barrage of pointless gossip that you had to pretend you were interested in hearing. The luthier was quick to take offense.

I started up my Škoda Felicia and out of the speakers I'd recently had installed came the voice of Susan Tedeschi singing *It Hurt So Bad*. Just then, I was listening to her a lot. I liked her, both as a singer and as a woman. I'd fallen in love with her more or less in the year 2000, watching one of her videos. She was accompanying Bob Dylan on a version of *Highway 61* that sent shivers down my back. She wore a good-little-girl dress and a pair of black flats. Nothing like the short red skirt worn by Ana Popović, another great love of mine. I couldn't believe that a young woman born in Belgrade would be capable of taking on the blues and, purely out of curiosity, I went to see her in concert in Munich in 2011. At the end of her solo rendition of *Navajo Moon* I was certain I wanted to marry her, but the infatuation ended quickly. My blues fiancée remained Susan Tedeschi, with whom I dreamed of spending the rest of my days. But now there was room in my heart only for the jazz woman who, unlike the American singer, lived in the same city as me and was far more attainable. I turned up the volume and shifted gears, thinking all the while about the story I'd just heard.

I'd turned down the job the Spezzafumo gang had offered me because, as clients go, they were dangerous, unpleasant assholes. The housekeeper, more than anyone else, deserved justice, but they didn't care. I would have liked to take on the case: Robbing private residences, staging violent home invasions that shattered lives, torturing people, murdering them— these were all odious crimes. The problem was finding the right client. Without someone hiring me, I couldn't justify my interest. The rules needed to be respected.

Max was snoring on the sofa with a book balanced on his gut. I woke him up and brought him up-to-date. He listened, paying close attention, before starting to reason through each element.

"Caution," he said, before going back to sleep. "The one sensible word to repeat like a mantra is: caution."

Knowing him, that meant that the story hadn't made much of an impression on him. I, on the other hand, thought about nothing else until I finally collapsed into sleep in front of the television.

* * *

A small workshop, five workers, a "storefront" carved out of small room next to an office that must once have been a broom closet. *Maglificio Gigliola*, clothing in genuine cashmere. Gigiola Knitwear. The idea for the name must have been the late Gastone's. His framed photograph stuck out on a desk cluttered with paper.

"Whatever it is you're selling, I'm not interested," the widow said clearly in a weary voice.

Gigliola Pescarotto had no doubt once been an attractive woman. Now her features were drawn taut, almost to their breaking point, with heartache, and she'd stopped taking care of her appearance the moment she'd found her husband's corpse. She'd become a portrait of the tragedy she was living.

"My name is Marco Buratti. I specialize in somewhat unusual investigations."

"What you mean by unusual?"

"The kinds of cases no licensed investigator would dream of taking," I explained. "Yesterday evening Nick Spezzafumo asked me to look into the armed robbery and double homicide. I turned him down."

The woman paled. "Nicola? What did he tell you?" she demanded suspiciously.

"Everything. Or almost," I replied, just to make sure she understood she could trust me.

She shook her head bitterly. "All he cares about is the gold and getting revenge. He doesn't understand that if he keeps trying to find the bastards who murdered Gastone and Signora Luigina, we'll all wind up in prison," she said, all in a rush. "And I don't want to lose my daughter. Lara is all I have left. She's the reason I find the strength to get up every morning and come down here to break my back."

"In other words, you don't care about catching the murderers."

"I wish I could care, but I can't afford to."

"The housekeeper was an innocent victim, she suffered more than anyone. She, at least, deserves some justice, don't you think?"

A sob shook her chest. "Poor Luigina. She was so good, and so good at her job. A little strange, sure. She came to work for us because she needed some time on her own, time to recover and figure out what to do with her life after a string of disapointments.

"Her man had knocked her up and then dumped her for

some foreign woman he followed to Slovenia. She'd left her son, Sergio, with her brother when the boy was eight or nine, and she showed up at our house with an old suitcase.

"That night I'd asked her to come with us. I'd insisted, in fact, because it was the recital for the parish dance class, and for Lara it was a big deal. Gastone wasn't interested in that kind of thing, and it hurt the girl's feelings. But Luigina said that she still needed to get the kitchen straightened up and that the next morning she had to wash the curtains.

"It was the girl who found her. Naked, covered in blood. She screamed so loud it still makes my blood run cold. Then, when I found Gastone's body, it was my turn to scream."

She put her hands to her ears, touching them delicately with her fingertips. "I'm sorry about what happened to her," she continued. "I wish I could have died in her place. Luigina's murder was our fault. You can't imagine the remorse I feel. It eats away at me. But things have to stay the way they are."

"You said 'our' fault. Were you involved in your husband's criminal activities, too?"

She nodded. "From the very beginning," she replied. "And not because I loved Gastone and had sworn at the altar to share everything with him. Gold is a disease and it entered my blood. I enjoyed it when Nick and my husband melted down the jewelry and turned the metal into tiny ingots that I then had to weigh. That was my job. Every gram meant money. We would have had to be patient for a few more years, and keep a low profile, do our best to make ends meet with the knitwear business, but then we would have left the country and that gold would have given us the good life. The kind of life that small businessmen being worked over by these government bloodsuckers can only dream of.

"It had never crossed my mind that things could go sideways. We were the best, the smartest, the most careful.

"We were wrong. It was all wrong. You should never get

mixed up with this stuff, not even for all the gold in the world, because if you do, fate steps in and punishes you.

"You understand? Not even for all the gold in the world."

I offered her a cigarette. She smoked it, pinching it between her thumb and forefinger, like a longshoreman.

"Do you have any idea how they found out about you?"

She stared for a few seconds at the ash at the tip of her cigarette before crushing it out in the ashtray. "Someone betrayed us. We were sold out," she said. "But I can't even imagine who it could have been, though I'm sure it was someone very close to us."

"How many people are we talking about? Three, four, five? I don't think it would be too much trouble to investigate them thoroughly."

"Nicola's already done that."

"It's not his profession. He certainly overlooked important clues."

She sprang to her feet. "This whole story is buried with the dead."

I sat there and gave her a long, hard look while I tried to come up with the right words to make her understand she was just kidding herself. "Nick Spezzafumo won't be satisfied with my refusal. Sooner or later the lid's going to come off this thing. Some stories you can never shake."

Province of Pordenone. The next day.

Near the main gate, the fence surrounding the well-known appliance factory was covered in dirty, tattered union signs and banners. They were all that remained in the wake of the strike's defeat. At the end of the shift, the few workers left trickled out and got into the cars parked on the other side of the road. Max and I were leaning against the side of a white Fiat Panda, smoking cigarettes. A man in a jumpsuit headed straight for us.

"That's my car!" he said in an aggressive tone.

"Are you Arnaldo Cantarutti?" I asked, extending my hand.

He refused to shake it. "Who are you?" he demanded suspiciously.

I pointed to my partner. "His name is Max, I'm Marco. We're private investigators and we're working on the robbery that resulted in your sister's death."

"Get out of here," he ordered. "You're not the first to try and cheat us out of our cash so you can pretend to investigate."

"We don't want your money," the fat man broke in. "We just want to talk about Luigina."

"Are you missionaries, do you work for free?" he mocked us as he pulled his car keys out of his pocket.

I decided to lie. "We were hired by a lawyer. A client of his had his house broken into by a gang of three men. He's convinced it was the same people who invaded Oddo's villa."

"Identifying the culprits also means obtaining damages," Max added. "In order to avoid life sentences without parole, these kinds of criminals are always inclined to indemnify their victims."

"They deserve to die for what they did to Luigina," the man muttered. "But it's also true that a little extra money wouldn't hurt. Ever since Sergio came to live with us, there's never enough money. At first she helped us out with her salary as a housekeeper, but after the funeral everything changed. I love the boy, but my wife isn't always so patient. He doesn't have any other relatives. His grandparents are too old and they're sick. Taking care of the boy always means depriving our own two kids of something they want. If this keeps up, we'll have to send him to an orphanage."

"One more reason to accept our help," I said, looking him straight in the eyes.

"I'm not signing anything," he retorted promptly.

Max flashed a door-to-door salesman's smile. "There's no

need. All we'd need is to chat for a few minutes about your sister."

The factory worker glanced at his watch. "There's not much to say. She was a good soul, a hard worker, but a little slow. I don't know if you get what I'm saying . . . She was attractive and men tood advantage of her. Sergio's father hit the road right away, he never meant to acknowledge the kid as his son. And Luigina never recovered. She tried to find another man who might really love her, but when Sergio turned eight she took a housekeeping job so she could get out of this town. The Oddo family was fond of her. They treated her respectfully and let her believe she was the governess while she was actually nothing more than a simple housecleaner who also did the cooking."

"She was a really good cook, you know?" he added after a short pause, lost in some memory. "Her mother taught her."

Luigina's life could be summarized in just a few words, many of them not especially flattering. Only as a cook was she really up to snuff. And yet, in that whole mess, she was the only one who deserved justice and reparations. I'd finally realized who our client could be.

"Do you think it might be possible for us to meet Sergio?" I asked.

"He never talks about what happened to his mother."

"Just for the report," the fat man lied. "Lawyers are always such sticklers."

Cantarutti shrugged. "At this time of day, he's at the parish church, kicking the ball around the soccer field."

The grass on the field grew in isolated clumps. The rest was bare dirt. The kids kicked up clouds of dust as thick as talcum powder. They were playing a game of pickup soccer, shouting and laughing. It was a pleasure to watch them. Our presence didn't pass unobserved. A man in his early thirties with a stack of photocopies under his arm and a gold cross around his neck strode toward us briskly.

"We'd like to talk to Sergio Cantarutti," said Max.

"We have his uncle's permission," I added, to stave off the usual questions.

The man gestured to a fair-haired boy to come over. "These gentlemen are here to speak with you," he explained, before heading off.

According to the only photo of her we had been able to find on the Internet, the boy took after his mother. Forehead, nose, the shape of his lips. But his eyes were dark. He wasn't tall, but he had broad shoulders. He seemed ill at ease.

"Can we buy you an ice-cream cone?" asked Max, pointing to the parish church café.

"I just want to go back to my game."

"All we need is five minutes of your time," I explained.

"What for?" he asked, suddenly curious.

"We're private investigators," I replied. "Like the ones in the movies. We want to find out who hurt your mother, but in order to be able to investigate, we need a client who'll give us a retainer, which means money to hire us. As the next of kin, that would have to be you."

Now he was frightened, uncomfortable. "Uncle Arnaldo says that we have to resign ourselves, that no one will ever figure out the truth."

"We're the best investigators on the market, and we're cheap, too," I retorted, holding out my hand. "Just hand over your spare change, and we can start working for you."

With clear misgivings, he stuck his hand in his pocket, pulled out twenty cents, and laid the coins on my palm.

Both Max and I solemnly shook his hand and a few seconds later he was already running to rejoin his friends.

As soon as we walked out the gate, Max touched my arm. "Are we sure we know what we're doing?"

"No," I replied in all sincerity. I showed him the coins. "But we do have certain responsibilities toward our client."

"Seriously though, Marco," he said; he'd stopped short and was refusing to go on. "Why are you dragging us into this fucked-up mess? The widow Oddo told us loud and clear she wants no part of this and that little boy may be sad as all hell, but he can hardly be considered a client."

"Maybe I just can't stand the idea of the truth staying buried," I snapped back, raising my voice, "or the idea that there's just one victim too many, with one child too many, and that they're liable to be shit out of luck for the rest of eternity."

"Got it," he blurted, and started walking again. "We can't just look the other way."

"We have our rules," I pointed out.

Max shot me an ironic little grin. "Remember who you're talking to."

"All right, okay," I said, giving in. "I need a case. A dirty, difficult, dangerous case. Otherwise I'll go to pieces, I'm already teetering on the edge."

"Then this one seems perfect to me," the fat man commented.

After taking Max home I continued on toward Vicenza. Edoardo "Catfish" Fassio, a real blues expert, the only true Italian "blue-jay," was spinning that night in a club in the provinces.

I got there early. Catfish was eating a bowl of pasta. He waved me over to his table.

"Everyone says the blues is dead but here we still are," he said as he poured me a glass of red.

"The blues just don't know how to give up."

We toasted to the devil's music and he took the opportunity to give me the once-over. "You've got the face of someone who's not going to make it unless he gets a horse-pill sized dose of good old-fashioned blues."

"I've been prescribing myself a lot of Susan Tedeschi."

"She's good and she's cute," he noted as he slid his hand into a bag he kept by his side, "but you need more powerful injections."

He set a few CDs down in front of me. His famous mixtapes. "Start with this," he added, pointing to one entitled *Night Stalker*, Missy Andersen's old warhorse.

"Thanks, Catfish."

He went and sat down at his booth onstage. A few minutes later, people were dancing as he put on records and recounted juicy anecdotes about the singers. All while repeating that people who didn't like the blues could go fuck themselves.

Two hours later he came back and sat down at the table, but by then I was too out of it to carry on a conversation. The owner knew me and let me sleep on a bench. When I woke up the next morning, I found the bartender restocking the bar. He made me an espresso and gave me a message from Catfish. "He paid the tab, but next time it's your treat."

"Big tab?"

He laughed before answering. "I haven't seen a drinker like you in quite some time."

I hoped that was a compliment, and lit the first cigarette of the day.

"You can take the alcohol out of the blues, but you can't take the blues out of the alcohol," I philosophized, trying to set a slightly more dignified tone as I headed for the door.

I began the round of therapy Catfish had prescribed by listening to the first CD, and by the time I opened the door to my home I felt oppressed by an unmotivated sadness. That's the way it works with the blues, you start over from the bottom and then you try to pull yourself back up.

"A woman?" the fat man asked; he was, as usual, engrossed with the day's papers.

"A bottle," I replied, heading for the bathroom. I needed a shower.

I took it slow, and gave up on the idea of shaving after a couple of misguided attempts. I was still pretty drunk.

When I got back to the living room, I was met with a bear hug from Beniamino. As usual, he was impeccably garbed. He was wearing a light wool, hazel brown, double-breasted suit, and a pair of leather shoes in bordeaux that looked quite expensive. The knot in his tie was perfect.

"Satisfied with your new boat?" I asked.

He smiled. "To call her a boat doesn't do her justice, but in any case, yes, I'm satisfied, and she's already earned me a few thousand euros."

"Have you gone back to smuggling?"

"If a good opportunity turns up, I won't let it pass me by."

Max uncorked a bottle of white wine. "I brought Beniamino up-to-date on the story that Spezzafumo told you."

I darted an inquisitive look in his direction. "Well?"

Old Rossini tasted the wine. "Nothing to write home about," he commented. "Exactly like this case. As far as I'm concerned, I'm pretty sure we have no real right to be digging into it, but it's also true that I've always hated those pieces of shit who do home invasions, and the housekeeper and her son have every right to fair retribution."

"So?" I insisted.

"We have to give it a try, but we can't hope for too much. If in two years neither the cops nor Spezzafumo found so much as a single clue, I doubt we'll be able to."

I heaved a sigh of relief. "So where do we start?"

"I know a guy who scouts out kidnapping targets in the Treviso area," Beniamino replied.

"Nice people you hang out with," Max kidded him.

"Wait until you see how happy he is to see us," Rossini snickered.

Toni Brugnera had never bothered to find himself a cover.

Everyone knew that he was supported by his wife, who owned a popular beauty spa. Between eleven in the morning and dinnertime, he could be found in any of a number of cafés and bars in the center of town, both recounting and collecting gossip. The gossip he liked best had to do with money, and how much of it people living in isolated villas had, especially if that money was being hidden from the tax authorities. And when he had hot gossip, Toni shared it with Nella Povellato, his longtime mistress, who, in turn, would turn it over to her daughter's live-in boyfriend, the Croatian gangster Franko Didulica.

Franko had a group of trusted friends who could cross the border, pull off a job, and get back home before the loot had even been missed.

Toni and Beniamino had met when the scout had gone to Beniamino to ask if a member of the gang, who'd been wounded in a shoot-out with a security guard, could hitch a ride in Beniamino's speedboat.

Rossini had turned down the job because he believed that cowards who assaulted defenseless families in their homes were true scum. Brugnera had raised his voice, and gone home with a face swollen from Rossini's fists. Didulica had threatened revenge, but he'd given that up once he realized it wasn't in his interest to make an enemy of the Italian who boasted dangerous friendships in Croatian smuggling circles.

That morning, when Toni walked out his front gate, he saw Beniamino step out of his luxurious sedan and invite him to come for a ride. And Toni turned white as a sheet.

"I'm not coming," he said in dialect as he bent over to peer inside the car. We both gave him a friendly wave.

"We just want to talk to you," the old bandit clarified. "Don't force me to hurt you."

The scout pointed to the corner of his building. "The video camera's filmed it all, so be careful."

"I see you've taken precautions," Beniamino commented

ironically. "And I can't blame you, what with all the sewer rats out there ready to rob the homes of respectable citizens."

The man got in back and sat down next to me. "What do you want to talk about?" he asked aggressively.

"What do you know about the robbery at the Oddo family's home two years ago?" I asked, point-blank.

"The place in Piove di Sacco?"

"Yes."

He raised both hands. "I didn't have anything to do with that," he said, still in dialect. "Two dead for fifty thousand euros' worth of swag—that's crazy. I'd always assumed that junkies did the job, but the fact that they never caught them made me change my mind. Maybe the robbery was cover for a revenge killing. I heard that Gastone Oddo liked exotic pussy."

"And who told you that?"

"It was a rumor that was going around at the time."

I exhaled loudly. That asshole didn't know anything useful.

"What crews were operating at the time?" Rossini asked.

"A dozen local scouts for a dozen gangs. Serbs, Bulgarians, Croatians, Romanians, Sinti, Neapolitans, and guys from Bergamo," he replied. "But believe me, none of them had anything to do with what happened."

Beniamino put on his blinker and pulled over. "Get out," he ordered.

Brugnera didn't have to be told twice; he walked off briskly, cursing us under his breath.

"So now we can be certain that the crews that specialize in robberies had nothing to do with that one," Max said.

"Spezzafumo's right. We're going to have to search for a one-off gang," I added, opening a new pack of cigarettes.

"And the traitor," old Rossini specified. "We need to go back and talk with Nick the Goldsmith or the widow."

"Better if we talk to Gigliola," I replied. "Spezzafumo and his boys have ugly intentions and if they find out we're digging, they'll demand to know what we've turned up."

At lunch, Gigliola Pescarotto, the widow Oddo, made do with a salad, half a liter of mineral water, and an espresso with two teaspoonsful of sugar. She ate lunch alone at a reserved table in a café that was just a few hundred yards away from the knitwear plant. Thanks to the twenty-euro note I'd slipped the waitress, on that day, she found her table occupied by yours truly and two men she'd never met before. I greeted her and waved her over.

"We'll be a little bit cramped but we need to talk with you," I explained after introducing Max and Beniamino.

"Are these gentlemen also aware of everything that happened?" she asked in a low voice.

"These are my partners. And my best friends," I replied, trying to reassure her.

"I'm not interested. I already told you I was done with this story."

"There are some new developments," I said. "We now have a client who's hired us to find out more."

"And who would that be?"

"Sergio, Luigina Cantarutti's son."

"But he's just a boy," she exclaimed, scandalized. "What kind of people are you, anyway?"

"Perfectly respectable," Beniamino said, cutting things short. "And in any case, you have no say in the matter. You need to trust us and give us all the necessary information."

She pushed her plate away with an angry gesture. "You're reckless fools. It'll be your fault when they take my little girl away from me."

"That won't happen," I retorted. "But speaking of children, Sergio's likely to wind up in an orphanage because his uncle doesn't make enough money to support him and his aunt doesn't want him living with them. You ought to meet him, he's a nice kid."

After the espresso, we went outside to smoke a cigarette. "What do you want to know?" the woman asked, her voice resigned.

"What would happen when Spezzafumo brought you the loot from the robberies?" Rossini asked.

"The jewelry was melted down into twenty- and fifty-gram gold bars."

"All of it?"

"The especially valuable pieces, those with fine stones, would be sold outside the country to a single fence, while the gold was parceled out to four others outside the Veneto region."

"Did they pay cash?"

"Always."

"And what became of the cash?"

"Some of it was divvied up among us, and the rest was invested in restaurants, bars, and cafés. We secretly financed quite a few places."

"Was Gastone in charge of that?"

"No, an old friend of ours was. He was Gastone's best man at our wedding."

"So you're not exactly going hungry."

"He bought us out for a ridiculously small sum," the woman admitted. "Our investor cut us loose. Fear and greed."

"Maybe he's the one who sold you out in the first place," Rossini announced. "Because one of these gentlemen definitely did it."

"Maybe the weak link is in Nicola's gang."

"I doubt it," I put in. "There's just three of them, and they do it all on their own. And then, there's no upside."

Gigliola crushed out her cigarette with the heel of her shoe. Max handed her a notebook. "We need names and addresses."

She was diligent and as accurate as she could be, but when she left, she didn't say goodbye.

One of the fences, Tazio Bonetti, was an old acquaintance of mine from prison. Like everyone in his line of business, there was no trusting him when it came to money, but he'd never posed any problems in terms of security. He lived in Brescia and, despite his initial surprise, he courteously feigned delight at being able to invite us to dinner in a venerable old inn, where a plaque listed Garibaldi among the illustrious diners from centuries past.

He showed up five minutes late. Actually, he'd gotten there half an hour early and peered in through the front door to make sure we didn't have some nasty surprise waiting for him. Fences' clients are never entirely happy with them. What with all the haggling over prices and the pretending that no one's interested in buying, from time to time, people lose their tempers.

He was a man in his early seventies, not tall, on the frail side, not a hair on his head. He was nicely dressed, though in a style very different from the one favored by old Rossini, to whom he immediately paid his respects. Then he shook hands with Max and, last of all, gave me a hug.

He overwhelmed us with dull and pointless chatter until the waiter served the wine, then he came straight to the point. "What do you want from me?"

"Gastone Oddo," I replied flatly, watching for his reaction.

He merely fluttered his hands, an untroubled gesture. "I miss him, may his soul rest in peace . . . I can't think what else to tell you."

"Have you come up any idea as to who might have ripped him off?"

"No. One of the many crews from the east, I'd imagine. They do plenty of home invasions in the countryside around here, too."

Beniamino chose to treat him with old-school courtesy. "Could we show you a list of people in your line of work and ask your opinion of each?"

"Just in case I know them."

"Just in case."

"First I'd like to understand what part you're playing in all this, and above all why you're interested in the fences who were working with Oddo."

"We can't answer that because we wouldn't want to show you any disrespect by trying to get some lie past you," Max replied promptly. "But we would like you to take us at our word: You have nothing to worry about. As far as your name goes, our lips are sealed."

Bonetti lowered his voice. "I'm not stupid, you know," he snapped. "You're convinced that one of us robbed Oddo."

"We're not all that sure of it, Tazio. We're just checking out every possibility."

"Spezzafumo already came to see me, and he asked the same questions."

"He likes to settle his accounts with a bullet to the brain," I retorted. "We have different objectives."

Rossini handed him the list. The fence put on his glasses and scanned it. "Don't waste time on Imbriani. He got out of the business shortly after the tragedy at Oddo's house."

Pierpaolo Imbriani, according to the information given us by Oddo's widow, Gigliola, had left Trieste thirty or so years ago and had moved to Belgium so he could marry a woman from Liège. He fenced the most valuable jewelry, the pieces that it would be a crime to melt down.

"Why did he do that?" I asked.

"It seems that his wife is sick, and he's devoting himself to her full-time."

"And what do you have to say about the others?"

He grabbed the sheet of paper and tossed it onto the table

with a testy gesture. "None of us would have allowed ourselves to get mixed up in such a miserable act."

He stood up. "I've just remembered an urgent commitment I can't put off, much less cancel," he explained, icily.

I blocked his way. "Do you realize that you're vouching for everyone but Imbriani? In a backhanded way, you've just put him right under the spotlight. Why?"

"The story about his wife was a fairy tale. That's all. Maybe he's got nothing to do with it."

"But that's not what you told Spezzafumo."

"I don't want dead men on my conscience."

Tazio had behaved sensibly and properly, and I was sorry he'd taken offense.

I invited him to stay, but he had absolutely no desire to. As soon as he was gone, the waiter arrived with our meal. "Won't the signore be dining?" he asked, stunned.

Max pointed at the table. "Go ahead and leave the food. We'll take care of it."

Beniamino shot him a glance. "Have you found a dietitian who recommends eating twice as much as usual?"

The fat man started telling him all about his experience with the last in a long series of nutritionists, but at a certain point, old Rossini interrupted him. "I was just kidding, Max. If you want to lose weight and live longer, just eat smaller portions; if you don't, eat all the fucking food you want. But don't come talk to me about holes in your life and all that bullshit from the seventies. Save that for Marco."

"Don't try and drag me into this," I protested.

"You pipe down. You're getting us into this mess to keep from losing your mind. The two of you are so off when it comes to mental balance that you're like a couple of tightrope walkers."

"And you're A-OK in that department?" I asked tartly.

"No. By no means," Rossini replied calmly. "But I do my

best to go on living without busting anybody else's balls. The two of you, on the other hand, are a pair of unbearable whiners."

I couldn't help but laugh. "But you have to agree that Max is much more of a whiner than I am."

"That's not true," the fat man said, defending himself, as he reached for the risotto the fence had ordered.

* * *

Liège.

I left the hotel shortly before noon and walked down the Boulevard d'Avroy with an Italian newspaper under my arm so I could be identified. Beniamino and Max had gone ahead in a rented compact car, but just then I couldn't spot them. A sedan pulled up beside me and I got in back. The driver was a silent young man who started driving in the direction of downtown, though not to any precise destination. He couldn't have been any older than twenty-five but he was already balding and the goatee he was clearly proud of was devoid of distinction. He kept sneaking glances at me in the rearview mirror; his eyes were dark and evil. He wanted me to understand that he was meaner than me and that violence was his daily bread. I guessed he probably wasn't that tall, but his arms bulged with gym-hardened muscles.

After a while, I grew tired of that buffoonery. "Let me out of the car," I demanded.

His only response was to take a picture of me with his cell phone and send it to someone who clearly needed it to recognize me. Someone who had to be Pierpaolo Imbriani. After a few minutes, he stopped outside the Café Lequet in Quai-Sur-Meuse.

"You can go now," he said in a Pugliese accent. The asshole was Italian.

I stopped to look at the river. The waters of the Meuse seemed as thick as molasses and flowed sluggishly. I took advantage of the moment to look around. All seemed calm.

As soon as I walked in, a man of about fifty sitting at a table raised one hand so I'd see him. In jeans and a brand-name polo shirt, he looked more like a tourist than a respected jeweler.

I stuck out my hand and introduced myself. "It hasn't been easy getting your attention."

Imbriani remained impassive. "As I've tried to explain to you several times without success, I'm no longer interested in acquiring certain merchandise."

I pulled out my cell phone and showed him pictures of authentic Art Nouveau-style bracelets, rings, and brooches in white gold and sapphire. "They're impossible to trace. The product of some clever sleight-of-hand in a contested inheritance," I explained. Actually, they'd belonged to Sylvie, Rossini's woman, and they weren't for sale just now.

The jeweler gave me back my cell phone. "This place is famous for its *boulet* meatballs and french fries."

I took a look around. An old café, furnished in sixties style, with posters on the wall reminding patrons that Georges Simenon was born not far away.

"Let's have the specialty of the house," I said.

He caught a waiter's attention and ordered for us both.

"I could be interested," he muttered. "It all depends on the price, of course."

The time had come to cast off the mask. "Before we start negotiations, there's another matter we need to clear up."

He turned watchful. He was starting to smell rip-off. "Which would be what?"

"There's someone who thinks it was you who plotted against Gastone Oddo."

It was the sudden dismay that gave him away. He didn't even try to regain his composure. He stammered out a fairly unconvincing defense. "You're wrong. I had nothing to do with that."

"But right after the home invasion and the murders, you decided to retire."

"My wife was sick."

"That's a lie. We checked it out."

"All the same, I had my reasons."

We were interrupted by the arrival of our drinks. Imbriani drank down a long gulp of beer.

"You have a major problem," I started to explain calmly. "If you don't tell me the truth or persuade me you had absolutely nothing to do with it, I'll go back to Italy and give your name to Oddo's partners.

"And someday you'll have to confront them. They'll use the same treatment on you and your wife that was used on Gastone and his housekeeper. Torture and death. If you think that lackey you use as a chauffeur is capable of protecting you, you're making the last in a line of mistakes."

"I'm ready to run that risk," he hissed as he got to his feet. "You're accusing the wrong person."

I watched him leave. These days, it seemed like no one wanted to share a table with yours truly. I ate unhurriedly, satisfied that I'd identified the traitor. The meatballs and french fries lived up to their reputation. I ordered another beer before paying the check and leaving.

I barely had time to light my cigarette before I found myself face-to-face with the lackey from Puglia. "Pierpaolo doesn't want you here. Get out, and don't come back."

"You seem like an actor. How many times have you practiced that line in front of a mirror?"

I didn't even see the right hook that caught me on the chin; before I knew it, I was flat on the ground. He had just enough time to deliver one sharp kick to my ribs before Beniamino's elbow shattered his nose. The youngster was certainly stronger and faster than the old bandit, but he didn't have the necessary experience to face a professional who'd apprenticed as a street brawler and then refined his combat techniques in prison. Rossini worked like a blacksmith with a mallet and didn't stop until he felt certain that the lesson wouldn't soon be forgotten.

Imbriani's enforcer had dared to hit a friend of his, and now he'd paid the price. Max helped me to my feet. "I'm fine," I lied. I was in a lot of pain, but this was hardly the time or place to start complaining.

By the time we left, a small crowd had gathered to watch the show, though it hadn't lasted more than a minute. The slyest member of the crowd tried to sneak a picture, but his cell phone went flying into the river Meuse.

We reached the rental car and found refuge in the botanical garden, blending in among the other visitors. One of those places the cops never think to check. The knuckles of Beniamino's right hand were swollen. He put the hand under the cold spray of a fountain for a few minutes.

"You got here just in time," I said. That was my way of thanking him.

"But I stopped pounding on him too soon."

"Did you want to kill him?" Max blurted out in horror.

"Of course not," he replied. "But professional heavies are people who aren't right in the head, they need to be punished and stopped before they become genuinely dangerous. Sooner or later they cross the line into murder, and they develop a taste for it."

We were the last to leave. We ate dinner in an out-of-the-way restaurant and then went to the movies to watch an Italian film that had recently competed at Cannes. Only after one last drink for the road did we head back to the hotel. Max called the reception desk and asked for us, and we watched for the reaction of the desk clerk from across the street. He hadn't looked around, he hadn't even looked up.

He just went back to watching a soccer match on TV. In the end, Imbriani and his sidekick hadn't reported us to the cops. I could finally collapse onto my bed, switch on one of the RAI TV channels, and watch an extremely boring talk show about the regional elections in Italy that had been held the day before.

The most significant piece of information had to do with Veneto, where the party in favor of defending the territory's alleged rights had won in a landslide. A victory that jeopardized our future.

I called Max, who thanked me. "I needed to share a few thoughts I've had with someone."

"I'll settle for the condensed version."

He fell silent as he searched for the right worlds. "The privilege of our generational defeat is that we aren't forced to take part in this farce."

"The people are sovereign," I reminded him.

"And right now, we're no longer part of the people. Light-years separate us, and we're following paths that run in two opposite directions."

I wished him goodnight and changed the channel. I found a program promoting revolutionary exercise equipment that, if used for an hour every week, could firm and sculpt every single muscle. Especially the abdominals. I fell asleep after a few minutes.

We were staying in a chain hotel not far from the cathedral. The rooms were brutally rational, carefully designed down to every last detail to provide comfort equivalent to the price, and no more. Conceived to house guests overnight and spit them out in the morning, after a quick shower and a frugal breakfast.

I was dunking a croissant in my *caffè latte*, and in the background, Johnny Cash was singing *A Boy Named Sue*, a renowned talking-blues piece recorded at San Quentin penitentiary. Beniamino had already left to return the rental car and rent out another one from the competition and Max was still snoring. Then I saw Pierpaolo Imbriani come in.

I pointed him to the chair across from me and went on with my morning croissant-dunking ritual. I've never given much of a damn about food, I've always preferred alcohol, but this particular way of breakfasting always brightened my day.

I ran the napkin over my mustache. "I'm pleased to see that you're an influential person in this city," I pretended to compliment him. "It didn't take you long to find me."

He sighed. "Jewelers do a great many favors and only rarely ask for any in return. Which means it's easier to get a hard one when you need it."

The fence was playing the part of the wise man in too irritating a fashion for me to let him go on. "I'm astonished by your visit. My friends and I were already working on convincing you to continue that conversation of ours."

"I'm sure you were. That's why I'm here," he said. He looked around before going on.

"I can't stand violence," he hissed quietly. "It horrifies me. I can't handle it. What happened yesterday makes it clear to me that I need to get out of this mess as soon as I can, and once and for all."

I wasn't especially good at dealing with violence myself, but over time I'd learned to appreciate its necessity. I'd also gotten used to seeing it up close without getting too upset. But I'd never—never—be able to raise a hand in anger or pull a trigger. Max was just like me. Luckily, we had Beniamino, who knew how to be lethal and who protected us, sweeping away our enemies. Without him, we'd both have long been dead.

"I'm an easygoing professional who's always demanded that his jewelry not be stained with blood. It's a condition of my work," Imbriani continued. "I was very clear with Gastone, too.

"Then one morning in the shop, when there were no customers and my wife and I were arranging a new collection of jewelry, a guy came in, a Venetian. He spoke a mix of Italian and dialect, and he showed me an extremely finely made bracelet. Do you know anything about jewelry, Signor Buratti?"

"No."

"Then I won't bother you with the details. In any case, it was a magnificent piece, and I knew it very well because Gastone Oddo had sold it to me. I, in turn, had sold it to a Dutch colleague who, per our understanding, was supposed to place it in Dubai. But he didn't always do as he promised, and he'd made the foolish mistake of displaying in his window."

"The guy recognized it and he forced the Dutchman to give him your name," I summarized. I was in a hurry to understand what the story was, and Imbriani was a little slow with his exposition.

"He seemed like a bomb about to go off. He was stifling a rage so intense that he had a hard time talking."

"So what did he tell you?"

"That his brother had died on account of that bracelet," he replied, looking me in the eyes. "And that unless I told him the name of the man who sold it to me, he was going to kill me right then and there.

"I tried to reason with him, but he grabbed my wife by the throat and started squeezing, ordering me to talk. I was sure he was about to kill her."

"The name was all he wanted?" I asked.

"Yes, he opened the door and disappeared."

"Why didn't you warn poor Oddo?"

He looked down. The moment of shame had arrived. "Fear. My wife had a hard time recovering. And resentment. Gastone hadn't respected our agreement; he'd put us in danger."

Bullshit. Business partners don't treat each other like that.

His silence had cost an innocent woman her life. "What's this guy's name?"

"I don't know."

"Then I'll need the footage from the video camera in your shop."

"We're in Liège, Signor Buratti; here, discretion counts for more than security does."

"Can you at least describe him for me?"

"Forty years old, average height, light brown hair; he wasn't ugly, but his face was creased and tired."

"Is that all?"

"His hands," Imbriani added. "They were callused and beat-up."

I stared into his eyes for a moment, trying to figure out if he was trying to trick me with that bullshit, but he seemed satisfied with his shrewd description.

I went back to my cup of *caffè latte* without saying another word. I wouldn't even look at him. After a little while the fence stood up; he left a photo of the bracelet and headed off, mumbling a farewell.

Johnny Cash had just started in on *Bonanza*, the theme song from the famous TV series. Famous for me and the people of my generation, I mean. I'd never missed an episode, and it was quite a while before it dawned on me that those cowboys, with their sound principles, had none of the allure of real pioneers. They were nothing but members of a clan, forever fighting to defend their patrimony.

I wondered if the guy who had extorted Oddo's name out of that idiot Imbriani was part of a clan.

* * *

Padua.

We'd returned the night before from Belgium with a decidedly flimsy lead from a treacherous, untrustworthy man. Max would follow up on it. Beniamino had gone back to his speedboat and I'd gotten up early to go meet Cora.

The jazz woman was reading the paper, glancing at her cell phone every now and then to check for texts or see what time it was. I went over to her table, flashing a smile.

"What's the first thing a jazz singer does when she wakes up?" I asked.

The woman sighed. "She gets up, gets dressed, and goes home."

I took a seat next to her without being invited. "I apologize for that sleazy musician's joke but I didn't know how to strike up a conversation."

"Doesn't it seem a little early to be bothering a lady?"

"A lovely lady," I emphasized. "But anyway, yes, this is hardly the ideal time of day, but last night I couldn't come to Pico's. Otherwise I would have declared myself at just the right moment."

She eyed me carefully. "Now that you mention it, your face isn't new to me."

"We've seen each other here, too, sitting at adjoining tables."

She held out her hand. "Cora, pleasure," she introduced herself briskly. "And now I'd like to go back to reading my newspaper."

I ignored her words. I'd made up my mind to play the game out to the very end. "I know that you took voice lessons at my friend Maurizio Camardi's school, and I also know your real name: Marilena."

"And which name do you prefer?"

"Cora. To me, you're only Cora, in a green dress with green shoes. Jazz woman."

She seemed to like what I'd said, but her silence muffled my enthusiasm. I stood up to stave off further embarrassment. "I believe we'll meet again in this café. You're always welcome to share my table should the fancy strike."

"Do you actually like me, or do you just think it's worth giving it a try because I must be 'easy,' like all jazz singers?" she asked suddenly, touching her hand to her cheek.

"I like you a lot, more than a lot," I said with conviction. "It's been quite a while since a woman made my head spin like this."

"No kidding," she replied, her tone ambiguous; then she went back to reading.

I stood there looking at her in silence for a few seconds. No doubt about it, Cora knew how to floor a guy. I left the café stumped, but definitely more in love.

I swung by home. Max was sitting at his computer and gestured to me that he still hadn't found out anything.

I put in my earbuds to continue the treatment Catfish had prescribed. The second CD was entitled *I'm In Deep*, after the song by the Altered Five Blues Band. The music made me particularly clear-minded and capable of analyzing my encounter with my Cora. It didn't take me long to realize that this was a complicated situation. On the one hand, I couldn't tell her the truth because that would mean betraying my pact with her husband. On the other, it was wrong to start a relationship based on a lie. Luckily, at the moment, the chance of anything really happening was decidedly slim and I had all the time I'd need to rack my brain for a solution. For the nth time, circumstances were against me. And that couldn't be an accident. I was slipping inexorably into a wallow of self-pity when I saw the fat man coming toward me with a worried grimace.

"I want seafood," he announced. "I've already talked to Beniamino. We'll go to Punta Sabbioni, hop on his speedboat, and head for that little restaurant we know in San Pietro in Volta."

"You don't look like somebody who's in the mood to celebrate."

He shook his head decisively. "No. We've always worked twisted cases, but this one is the worst yet."

"Obviously on the way over you'll tell me all about . . ."

"No," he said, cutting me off. "When you tell a story twice, there's always a chance you'll leave out crucial details. Plus, I need to think."

Max was a man of his word. He split a pack of cigarettes with me, but said not a word—except to complain that it made no sense to spend a small fortune putting a stereo system into a car so old it didn't even have air conditioning.

June had come, dragging with it a mantle of oppressive heat. I promised I'd talk to the mechanic, even if I already knew the answer.

Beniamino was fresh from a night on the high seas. He'd transported an old fugitive who, after many, many years in Bulgaria, had decided to come back and turn himself in to the cops—though not until after he'd seen his two daughters.

"It broke my heart," said Rossini. "He looked like a homeless bum. He'd calculated his pension wrong, and going on the run has its costs."

"Then where did he find the money to pay you?" I asked, knowing the fares my good friend charged.

Old Rossini opened his eyes wide in surprise. "The passenger traveled gratis, Marco."

Of course. I should have guessed. The outlaw heart and its rules. I apologized; I'd opened my mouth without thinking.

To lighten the mood, Max started in on the air conditioning.

"This love affair of yours with old Škodas is the affectation of a radical-chic old schoolmarm," Beniamino piled on as *Sylvie*'s powerful engine roared to life.

I refrained from responding. We were all tired, on edge, and worried about what the fat man was about to tell us.

Luckily, the trip was short and agreeable. The water was calm and a slight westerly wind provided a perfect antidote to the heat.

I was always happy to go to San Pietro in Volta, a charming little town on Pellestrina, one of the largest islands surrounding Venice. I liked lazing on the benches or walking along the waterfront. It was a place where time went by at a different pace.

That day, after tying up, we immediately slipped into a well-known restaurant. In silence, we ate our antipasti, which had been paired with an ice-cold white pinot.

When the waiter took our plates away, announcing the arrival of the *risotto agli scampi* in just five minutes, Beniamino turned to Max with an impatient gesture. "So, what have you found out?"

"The man who roughed up Imbriani and spouse in Liège to get Oddo's name is called Kevin Fecchio, forty-three years old, a goldsmith by profession.

"The company in the Vicenza area where he still works was founded by his older brother Maicol—that's the Venetian version of Michael. Maicol was considered a real artist and he was the one who designed a successful line of jewelry, starting with the bracelet that wound up in Imbriani's hands. Business was going well, in fact it was booming, until the day that three armed robbers burst into the workshop and cleaned the place out. Before they made their getaway there was a struggle, and Maicol caught a large-caliber bullet in the gut. Kevin and the other employees were tied up and couldn't get help to him in time. He died after many hours in excruciating agony."

"Spezzafumo and his boys killed Maicol, so his little brother took revenge by murdering Oddo and his housekeeper and carting off two million," I summed up.

"That's exactly what seems to have happened," Max the Memory confirmed.

I turned to catch Beniamino's gaze. He was as flabbergasted as I was. The hand of a goldsmith, a businessman, might be behind the massacre in the villa. It was hard to believe.

"And that's not all," Max preempted us. "Kevin is now a prominent figure. Not only has he gotten the company back on its feet, he's also an activist in that more-or-less grassroots political movement protesting the lack of public safety. He's one of the first who leapt to defend the deli owner who shot and killed the would-be robber of Sinti origin a few months ago."

The fat man turned on his tablet and showed us Fecchio's Facebook page. He had a lot of followers. I skimmed the comments. It was the unfiltered voice of the Venetian heartland expressing itself. The voice that could be heard on television, read on the front pages of the newspapers. Mayors who were hailed for declaring that the Roma had no right to stay in their towns. Shopkeepers who fought back by opening fire, killed would-be robbers, and became heroes. Torchlight parades, T-shirts. Fear, exasperation, hatred. Lynch mob moods. And votes: So many votes that they ended the argument.

"Is he trying to land some political office?" I asked.

"Not at the moment. But he's truly tireless when it comes to organizing."

"Excellent cover if he really was involved in the robbery at the Oddo home," Rossini commented.

"Do you have any doubts?" Max asked, astonished.

"A few," he replied. "Why didn't he go to the police? After all, he's a civilian and his name never circulated in armed robbery circles. Nicola Spezzafumo would have caught wind of it."

The old gangster wasn't wrong. "We can always ask him," I suggested faintly, guessing at the eventual meeting's real reason: figuring out our role in all this and deciding what to do next.

Rossini shrugged. "It seems to me we don't have any other choice if we want to get to the truth."

"Kevin Fecchio is a public figure. We have to be very careful," the fat man broke in.

"Then we need to know more and that's your job," I retorted.

A smile stretched across the fat man's face. He couldn't wait to get to work.

Old Rossini poured a round of drinks with a thoughtful air. "Spezzafumo and his henchmen are truly nasty people. That Maicol bled to death; very probably, he could have been saved. There's no need to kill anyone just to steal some gold.

"And after all, if you wind up shooting some poor bastard in the guts just because you don't know how to handle the situation, it means you're not that good at what you do, and it's time to retire."

I felt a shiver run down my spine. "Are you planning to express your point of view to him?"

"At the first opportunity that presents itself," he replied indignantly. "They need to find a new line of work before they start more trouble."

I shot Max a look. This was proof that the job wasn't going to be painless, and that someone was definitely going to get hurt.

We dropped the subject and, when it was time to head back, Beniamino took the long way around. The *Sylvie* seemed to wander over the waves. Stretched out in the prow of the boat, we enjoyed a picture-postcard sunset, shooting the breeze as if we were little kids. Late that evening, I found myself in a nightclub, talking about my Cora with a Colombian hostess. We were in the mood to share personal stories. I told her about my romantic sorrows, she confided that she was flying a virgin cousin over and trying to place her on the bridal market. She wasn't sure what percentage she should take as a commission.

Rossini drank vodka in silence in the company of another

"girl" who would most likely be forced into retirement soon. She'd been a friend of Sylvie's back when Sylvie had danced in that same club, on the stage that the old gangster was looking at now, lost in his thoughts.

Max of course was ranting on about diets with other girls who had no customers to take care of. They were amused and laughing. When he wanted to, the fat man could deploy a self-deprecating irony whose comic beats were as good as any actor's.

If we'd been younger, we might have—with a dash of imagination—resembled a trio of soldiers about to head back to the front or sailors getting ready to set out for the China Seas. Instead, we were just waiting to walk through the darkness of crime and lies, in the hope that the truth might help us to set matters straight.

Max the Memory didn't take long to track down someone he could chat with about Kevin Fecchio. The man was a union organizer who had also known Maicol very well. The fat man had met this guy in the movement, when politics was by and large a matter of dreams. They'd since drifted out of touch, but a mutual respect had remained intact.

We met him early one morning at a pastry shop in Creazzo, in the province of Vicenza, a place known for the quality—and size—of its brioches.

Enzo, skinny and sick and tired of no longer being able to properly represent workers who were ever more discontented as their jobs grew ever more precarious, was very useful in giving us a sense of the world in which the Fecchio brothers moved.

Maicol was an entrepreneur in the true sense of the word. He'd built his company according to a precise plan that he'd continued to successfully expand until the day of his death. He had a dozen or so full-time employees with full benefits, and when he was under pressure to meet his orders he, like everyone else, paid freelancers under the table.

Kevin, according to the union organizer, was a hard worker and an immensely likeable person, who'd grown up in the shadow of his older brother. Maicol's death had completely transformed him. He'd turned aggressive; it had become impossible to have a reasoned discussion with him. For a couple of years the company had teetered on the brink of bankruptcy, not so much because of specific problems related to Maicol's death, but because Kevin had been unable to cope. Except for two of Kevin's childhood friends, everyone else had been fired. And his private life hadn't been going much better: His wife had left him, taking the children with her.

Then, suddenly, there had been a turning point. Fecchio had managed to get back on his feet and revive his company.

Max tactfully probed to flesh out the timeline, and the union organizer was able to be fairly precise: The winds had started blowing in the company's favor three months after the armed robbery at the home of Gastone Oddo.

As the evidence piled up, Kevin was becoming more and more interesting. The fact was that there was little doubt he'd been involved—but we were neither cops nor judges. We needed solid proof before we could present the check.

"I've heard he likes to play sheriff," I tossed out, pretending I just wanted to make conversation.

Enzo lowered his voice: "He watched his brother die without being able to lift a finger to help him; the pain and grief sucked him dry of everything good he'd ever had in him."

The union organizer had guessed that our interest in Fecchio went beyond the company and asked us if we needed to know anything in particular.

"We need to get in touch with him," Max replied. "But we don't know how. We ought to have a thorough knowledge of his private life but we don't have time."

The man made a baffled face. "He lives for his work and for the 'cause.' In his free time he always and only sees two friends, Sante Zanella and Vasco Merlin. But to be perfectly honest, there's not much more I can add. After all, we move in completely different circles."

"Are the other two men married?" I asked, following up on a hunch.

"Married with children, small-town life, the parish church, foosball, cafés. Normal guys."

Once we were alone, we went out to smoke a cigarette. By then I had half an idea about how to continue our investigation. "A young man who works all damn day and spends his time with a group of good citizens whose politics are a little over the top, a man who wants to take justice into his own hands and who no longer lives with his wife—this young man, who does he fuck? Maybe he also runs with a more unusual crowd."

"Are we really interested in finding out?"

"I think we are. Kevin Fecchio is the knot tying this whole case together. A chat with him is inevitable and urgent. And maybe by following this path, we can find a suitable situation."

The fat man opened his hand, and I placed the cigarette pack in it. "Explain yourself," he said.

"He's not yet forty-five and I don't believe he's given up sex. But at the same time, he's a public figure and he has to be careful. If you ask me he has some nice relaxed arrangement he can count on. An arrangement he's paying for."

"Maybe he's found a girlfriend," Max objected.

"That news would be public domain by now."

My partner wasn't completely convinced. "Do you have someone in mind who can help us?"

"Yes, but I'll go alone."

He flashed me a mischievous smile. "And why would you want to do that?"

"You aren't her type. She wouldn't talk to you."

The world of prostitution is a complicated one, capable of adapting itself to the needs of the market. There's the street and the nightclub network. Then there are the Chinese women, set up in apartments, always available, 24-7. They work as intensely as they did in the clandestine sweatshops from which they were recruited. But there are potential customers who have trouble going out at night, whose family life makes that impossible, who have to carve out an hour in the morning or the afternoon, maybe on their lunch break.

For this specific sector of her clientele, Cinzia Donato had dreamed up and organized in Vicenza and the surrounding towns a network of housewives eager to earn good money, by and large leaving their legally wedded spouses in the dark.

Two women, never too young, per apartment, shifts of six to eight hours at the most. Discretion, select Italian clients, reasonable prices.

Those who might have problems calling their time and money their own were officially employed in boutiques, dressmakers' shops, millineries.

Cinzia had a very modern and managerial concept of her profession. The women who worked for her were treated like professionals, and she did everything she could to make them feel comfortable. Above and beyond a discreet system of video surveillance, security was handled by a pair of experienced guards who could, if needed, count on their numerous acquaintances in law enforcement for help.

Relations with the bigwigs were managed by the owner of the operation, and by her alone. Among the high rollers were politicians, industrialists, and the usual crowd of prominent men in the cities of the province—people who constituted, in Veneto, a real institution.

I'd first met Cinzia Donato when she'd hired me to track down a nephew who'd gotten mixed up with the wrong people.

A story with a happy ending: The boy was now doing well at some foreign university whose name I couldn't remember.

The madam received me in an office tucked away in the back of a boutique on the ground floor of an ancient palazzo in the heart of Vicenza's historic center. French windows gave onto an interior garden, large and well tended. She was sipping a drink in the shade of an oversized canvas umbrella. She was approaching sixty by now and she'd never really been pretty, what with her coarse features and thin lips, but she had eyes of an intense blue that made her face interesting. As always, she was dressed with refined elegance. That morning she was wearing a white dress with light-blue horizontal stripes and sandals in the same color. She could easily have been taken for a wealthy French matron.

"It's hot out," she said as soon as she saw me. "And now that we've exhausted weather as a topic, you want to tell me what you're doing here?"

"Do you know Kevin Fecchio?"

"Yes."

"Is he a customer of yours?"

"No," she answered. Then she smiled and tilted her head to one side. "Would you like a *chinotto*?"

"I haven't had one of those in years."

"This one is special, it would be a mistake not to try it."

I gave in, though I continued to insist that I wasn't crazy about soft drinks.

She got up and opened a small refrigerator. The bottle was ice-cold and the brand was unfamiliar. This was doubtless something very exclusive.

"Why are you interested in this guy?" the woman asked. "I'm asking you because I happen to like Fecchio. I like the things he says. There are lots of armed thugs around and citizens need to be able to defend themselves without being hassled."

"And it's bad for business, too," I threw in with obvious but pointless sarcasm.

"The less crime there is, the better it is for the local economy," she shot back with total conviction. "And another thing, they need to clear the gypsies out of the city center. They're intolerable. They just bother people; there's no use for them. But let's get back to Fecchio: What do you want from him?"

"I have to persuade him to talk to me about something that happened, but I can't just go up to his front door and ring his doorbell."

She lit a cigarette. From the first puff, the filter was smeared with lipstick. "I can ask around."

"I'd be grateful."

"So grateful you'd return the favor?"

"Of course."

"What about the *chinotto*, do you like it?"

"You were right, it's good."

"It's organic," she explained, before dismissing me with a wave of her hand.

I was certain that if there was anything to be found out, Cinzia would be the one to find it. I informed Max and sat down at a bar to have a "good strong" long drink, as I'd instructed the waiter.

I received a phone call from Maurizio Camardi. He was on the train and was heading for Rome to play at the Bar Ergo on the Lungotevere.

He told me that the jazz woman had gone to see him at the music school to ask for some information on yours truly.

"I told her the truth," said the saxophonist.

"Which is?"

He snickered. "That you're a good-for-nothing."

"Well, you sure are a true friend."

He changed his tone of voice. "She's definitely interested but she seemed a little upside-down, a little fragile."

"I'll be careful."

"You're not the type for that."

"You're right," I admitted easily. "Among other things, I've had to refrain from telling her one important detail that threatens to ruin everything."

"Next week I'm playing with Marco Ponchiroli and Francesco Garolfi. Cora promised she'd come hear us. You could swing by," Camardi invited me.

"I don't think I'll wait that long," I retorted, checking the time.

I was the first customer to enter Pico's. I set myself up at the bar and got ready for my meeting with the jazz woman by ordering a couple of gin and tonics. There was no danger of getting drunk. The bartender had standing orders to skimp on the alcohol, to keep from knocking the clientele straight to the floor.

The piano player arrived. He was thirsty, so I bought him a round. He told me that Cora was getting ready and wouldn't be on for at least an hour.

I discreetly slipped him a fifty-euro note. "Would you go tell her that I'm waiting for her here and that I'd like to buy her a drink?"

"Why don't you go?" he shot back, pretending to be offended. "I'm nobody's errand boy."

"I know that very well. In fact, this money is just to get you to play a couple of songs outside of your usual repertoire."

He grabbed the bill. "Sorry, I misunderstood."

"No, I'm the one who should apologize to you. I failed to make myself clear," I said to put an end to that stupid little routine.

The piano player came back a few minutes later. "She'd like a Singapore Sling," he explained with a wink, "in her dressing room. With you."

I thanked him and put my order in at the bar. The piano player watched me, perplexed. "What is it?" I asked.

"I tried so many times with her that, in the end, I decided she was totally indifferent to sex. I'm curious to see if you can get her into bed."

"I assure you that, at the moment, all I want to do is talk."

He shook his head. "I know jazz singers, I've fallen victim to them all my life, and I'm willing to lay odds."

Cora was all ready to go on stage; her makeup just needed a little touch-up. She drank her cocktail in silence. Every now and then she looked over at me. She seemed uncertain and I did everything I could think of to put her at her ease.

"Camardi said that you were an all right guy and that you know how to listen," she said all of a sudden.

"He's a friend," I replied, thinking to myself that it was with her of all people that I was behaving badly.

"I like you, but I don't feel like throwing myself into an affair with one of those dull men you always meet when you're going through kind of a strange time in your life, know what I mean?"

"I think so," I replied cautiously.

"Then you need to listen to me because I have some things to tell you first."

"All right."

She lit a cigarette. "Do you know why a woman like me sings jazz twice a week in this dive?"

"I honestly can't even begin to guess," I answered sincerely.

"I'm a nurse and I work in the serious burns ward and I need some distance from that," she explained. "I love the work but I'm not made of steel, and you can never really get used to other people's suffering."

"I understand."

"I've never cheated on my husband, and now I'm ready to do it. I don't know if it's right or wrong but I want it to happen.

Our marriage isn't on the rocks and I love him as much as I ever did but I'm irresistibly attracted to you because you pursued me. You made me feel important. Is all that clear to you?"

"Yes."

"Then go to the bar and get me another cocktail. I'm suddenly thirsty."

"You don't want to know anything about me?"

"No. I was told that you're basically reliable but I'm afraid that it would be a mistake to dig any deeper."

She wasn't wrong about that, and I hurried over to the bar. The bartender was slow. To make the drink, he had to look up ingredients and portions in a manual that had definitely seen better days.

He caught the perplexed look on my face and tried his best to justify himself. "Everyone always asks for the same few things. Then along comes a customer who orders a Singapore Sling, the kind of refined specialties you'd learn at bartender's school, and I've always had to work, I've never had time for any of that bullshit."

"It's already the second one you've made tonight, maybe you'll start to get the hang of it."

He smiled, putting a mouthful of nicotine-stained teeth on display. It occurred to me that he was a rare bird; it used to be easier to run into smokers who didn't care what their mouths looked like.

That thought made me miss the bartender's retort, but I didn't bother to ask him to repeat it. I had better things to do.

"Do you know how to kiss?" Cora asked me after a long sip. "Like, really kiss, I mean."

"I'm a first-rate kisser. Anywhere you care to point me."

"You seem to think quite a lot of yourself, kid."

We didn't waste time cautiously exploring each other's bodies. Our tongues intertwined passionately, urgently. I licked her nipples very slowly, almost as if I meant to drive her to distraction, before grabbing her and lifting her onto the makeup table. My hand made its way under her skirt; it was exactly what I'd been yearning to do since the first time I saw her. She pushed my shoulders down and I found myself on my knees, my face buried between her thighs.

I took it nice and easy as if time was all ours and no one else's. Making love on that rickety makeup table was no simple task, but when the piano player knocked on the door to tell us that the concert was beginning, we were embracing, exhausted and happy.

"My dress is all rumpled," Cora laughed.

"No one's going to notice."

"Now get out of here, I have to try to fix my makeup."

Instead, I stayed for a while and watched her. I couldn't break away from her. Jazz woman. A complete mess, frightened, fragile, but she got up every morning and tackled a tough job, in a place where pain was always king, and its dominion went unchallenged.

"I like you," I said as I left her dressing room.

She looked at me in the mirror and smiled.

Cinzia Donato got back in touch just as the weather turned. She called midafternoon as the overstressed windshield wipers of my Škoda Felicia struggled nobly against a violent downpour.

She arranged to meet me at a house in Castelgomberto, just outside of Vicenza, at 7:45 P.M. on the dot. The madam had always been a stickler for punctuality.

I sighed. It had been a little more than twenty-four hours and I was already standing up my new girlfriend.

She was at work and I couldn't call her. I wrote her a text in which the word "sorry" appeared three separate times.

I turned around and, since I was definitely running early, I left the highway and drove to a multiplex. I had no idea which movie to watch so, basing my decision more or less on the showtimes, I chose a movie by an Italian director. A famous, multiple award-winning director. I'd always been deeply grateful to the auteur school of filmmaking, which had put me in touch with aspects of life I knew nothing about. I often left the theater shaken, sometimes filled with wonder. The movies fed me with stories of the civilian world, as we referred to it, and helped me to understand ordinary people. But I felt no envy. Their world was still one I didn't like. Unlike Max the Memory, I'd never cherished the dream of changing it. I preferred to live on its outskirts.

That afternoon I was sucked into a story of old age and death, told with great delicacy. I sat there as the end titles scrolled past and was the last to leave. I leaned on my car and smoked a couple of cigarettes, immersed in memories of my early life, the life that ended the day I wound up in prison. For the umpteenth time I came to the conclusion that families are complicated and that everything becomes clear only when it's too late. And then all you're left with is time to waste on your regrets.

"You can't change the past," I muttered under my breath, pulling open the car door and rushing to slip the third CD prescribed by Catfish into the player: *El Diablo*, after the song of the same name by the Low Society Band. Mandy Lemons had a voice that could send shivers down your spine. I'd dreamed of seeing her live for years.

The other nineteen tracks on the disk were all just as diabolical and bracing as the first, from Creole United's zydeco to River of Gennargentu's central Sardinian blues. The memories slipped from my mind. *El Diablo* had managed to persuade the past to grant me a truce.

The street that Cinzia Donato had directed me to was located right behind the town's main piazza; the number matched a small, two-story house squeezed between a bakery and a stationery shop.

I was met at the door by a woman who looked to be about thirty-five, cute, in jeans and a white T-shirt, without a speck of makeup. She said her name was Marika but she hastened to explain that she'd been born and raised in Veneto.

She led me to a living room whose furnishings were all new, with the exception of a ceiling lamp in Venetian-style crystal— the kind of thing that had been fashionable in the sixties. It clashed with the rest. It looked as if someone had forgotten to take it down.

Cinzia Donato was sitting comfortably on the sofa. She greeted me with a half smile. "Darling," she said to the mistress of the house, "tell my friend all about Fecchio."

Marika didn't have to be asked twice. "Kevin comes to see me three or four times a month, always late at night. While we're doing it he calls me Sabina, same as his wife, then he bursts into tears, calls her names because she took his children away from him, and holds me in his arms until he falls asleep."

A man in despair. The world was full of them. I shot a glance at the madam. "So?"

"If you have issues, you need to go to a specialist," Cinzia snapped, "not to a whore who is, quite obviously, not a therapist. She's a sex worker, a professional who gets paid by the hour, and what she offers is for entertainment purposes only. The fact is, you men are always trying to find a mother."

It crossed my mind that, in fact, you can't sleep with your arms wrapped around your shrink, but I decided this was no time to venture into idle chitchat. "When's the next time he's coming?"

"He made an appointment for Thursday night at ten o'clock," Marika replied.

"I'd prefer it if he found me waiting for him instead of you," I told her. "That way I can talk to him in peace and quiet."

"Not unless you fork over a thousand euros, which includes

the income she'll be foregoing and the temporary rental of the house, along with a guarantee that nothing unpleasant will happen," Donato stated in a decisive tone. "We're not interested in winding up in the papers. Bad publicity is no good for business."

"So she works for you now?" I asked.

"The minute we started talking we hit it off," Cinzia replied. "And after all, can't you see how pretty she is? She's perfect for my clientele."

Marika was radiant. In the end, we were all happy; we'd all gotten what we wanted.

The madam told me goodbye and reminded me that now I owed her a big favor. That was true. We'd finally get a face-to-face with Kevin Fecchio.

The next morning I found a cop waiting for me when I left my usual café-tobacconist. I appreciated his not insisting on being welcomed into my home; it showed great tact. I recognized him first and foremost by his unmistakable Hawaiian shirt. He was the only cop I knew who made a point of being impossible to miss. His name was Giulio Campagna, inspector in the armed robbery division at Padua police headquarters. His ways, just like his apparel, were overstated, and this had definitely thwarted his career. Actually, his manner was a kind of suit of armor meant to conceal his soul, which was perennially tormented. By life; by his profession. He was a good person who wanted to abide by his own rules without cheating. I was sure that he respected me, if in his own fashion, even though he'd made it clear in the past that he'd prefer to see me behind bars. The fact was that I'd forced him to rethink his own concept of the truth, and he'd never forgiven me for it.

"Buratti, you're just the person I've been looking for," he began, in a strong Venetian accent. "I've got a doubt that's been nagging at me since this morning."

I started to unwrap a pack of cigarettes, resigned to sitting through one of his goofy tirades.

"I woke up this morning thinking about how the ads for cryotherapy to eliminate hemorrhoids have completely vanished. Years ago the newspapers were packed with ads for clinics that promised to perform miracles by sliding a little piece of Siberia up your ass. I've pored over the local papers and I haven't found a single line about it. What happened? Does no one suffer from this exceptionally irritating pathology these days? Or did they simply figure out that the method was worth fuck all, and now the Italian peninsula is teeming with poor bastards whose rear ends are as red as a baboon's?"

The time had come to interrupt him. "And so you decided it would interesting to come and talk the issue over with yours truly."

He smiled and accepted one of my smokes. "If not with you, then who? You're the only person I know who's soon going to be in need of a miracle cure to keep from going to prison, which is where, after all, you deserve to be."

I pretended not to be alarmed. "I have to confess you've lost me there."

"Just go on confessing, Buratti, because you need to explain to me just why you feel the need to go around with a bunch of other ex-cons asking questions about a certain armed robbery."

I tried to guess. With Campagna, it was no good trying to deny something he already knew; someone had spilled the beans. Most likely it was the kidnapping scout from Treviso. "Toni Brugnera?"

He shook his head. "My informants are none of your business."

An indirect confirmation. For that matter, Toni wasn't built to face the harsh realities of prison, a place he'd carefully avoided up till this moment. In the end he'd be willing to rat out his own son-in-law. A gangster like Franko Didulica was a get-out-of-jail-free card.

I sucked down a couple mouthfuls of smoke while I tried to come up with a fairy tale credible enough to get this inspector off my back, but nothing came to mind.

"I know you're working on something underhanded," he said, touching the tip of his forefinger to the cell phone I had in my breast pocket. "Your landlines and cell phones are as silent as little fishes, which gave me a mischievous idea: cloned or encrypted phone numbers."

The cop's suspicions were certainly well-founded. We'd long ago learned to protect ourselves from wiretaps and we spent tons of money to make sure we were getting the best the black market in security devices had to offer us.

"I have a client," I told him, choosing to venture onto the treacherous ground of half-truths.

"Who?"

"You know I can't tell you that."

"Seeing that you're an ex-con with no P.I. license, you don't have the right to investigate in the first place, not even into the theft of an apple from a fruit stand in the piazza."

I blew out my cheeks. "Don't start in with that old story."

"It's my duty to put you on notice: You're committing crimes that will cost you dearly."

I blew out my cheeks even more emphatically. "You've been trying for two years and you haven't found a thing. Maybe we're just luckier than you."

He angrily flicked his cigarette butt between my feet. "I know the way you like to wrap up cases."

"Then stay out of it."

"I took a look at the case file. Back then I was on the drug enforcement squad," he explained. "It's one of those investigations that pisses you off, and I have a mountain of cases like that to digest, understand? If there's so much as a sliver of a chance of finding the bastards responsible for that bloodbath, I want to be the first one to know about it."

I offered him another cigarette. He turned it down with a brusque gesture.

"Well then, I'm the one who doesn't want you underfoot," I blurted out.

"What?"

"This is a case that can't be solved while respecting your laws."

"At the moment, those are the only laws in effect."

"Listen, Campagna," I began in a reasonable tone of voice. "You need to trust me. If we're right about this thing, it would be covered up and forgotten at the speed of light if it ended up in your hands."

"And what about in your hands?" he asked contemptuously.

"There's at least a chance of the case being taken care of in a way that's fair to the victims."

He stared at me thoughtfully. "And what would you get out of it? None of the relatives has enough money to afford a crew of high-paid good-for-nothings like you guys."

"The retainer was twenty cents," I replied, ignoring the insult. Campagna always tended to provoke when he was feeling uncomfortable.

"Have you decided to go in for charity work?"

"You wouldn't understand," I replied. "But we're on the right side of this one."

"You realize that you have no right to even say this kind of stuff to me, and that I'm not allowed to stand here listening to it?"

"Then get out of here and leave me alone."

"What I ought to do is bring you into headquarters and grill you good."

I shrugged. "You're the cop. Make up your mind what you want to do."

I'd put him in a bind once again and he was furious. But I was sure he'd registered the honesty of my words. He slunk off with a classic cop line. "For now I'm going to have to file away this delightful encounter in a corner of my memory; anyway, I know where to find you."

He turned on his heels and started to leave. Then he thought better of it. "If I get any more tips about your illegal investigation I'll go straight to my bosses and I'll repeat every word of our conversation."

I nodded. And the inspector finally blended into the crowd of pedestrians hurrying along the sidewalk, their heads tucked down between their shoulders.

Campagna wasn't going to interfere, not unless he was absolutely forced to. I was sure of it, and I remained sure of it all morning, until I decided there was no need to tell my friends about my back-and-forth with the cop. It would only needlessly alarm them. Max hated the guy and Beniamino had never met him. I was the only one who could calmly judge the situation. And after all, we couldn't afford to waste precious time while we waited to meet Kevin Fecchio.

* * *

Edoardo "Catfish" Fassio was right: The blues outlived everything. Fashions came and went but the devil's music kept being played everywhere, and by great musicians. While waiting for some dramatic development in the investigation, I went to hear Fabrizio Poggi and his Chicken Mambo.

The evening was hot, the slightest movement brought rivulets of sweat, and beer oozed out of your pores along with it, but no one could resist the rhythm of *The Blues Is Alright*.

The lawn in front of the stage was teeming with cheerful, carefree people. I couldn't relax, I was dancing to absorb energy so I'd be strong enough to confront monsters and phantoms and dangerous unknowns like Kevin Fecchio.

I bought the CD and at the end of the concert stood diligently in line to get it signed. It was entitled *Spaghetti Juke Joint* and it was dedicated to those Italian emigrants who were victims of a gigantic fraud and found themselves in the cotton fields outside of Greenville, Mississippi, at the end of the nineteenth century, sharing the terrible living conditions of the African Americans. Slavery had been abolished but the Ku Klux Klan made the laws, and exploitation and disease had hardly vanished.

According to Poggi, we Italians had been in the right place when the blues was "invented." Legend tells of a club just off Tribbett Road, on the Dean Plantation, where on Saturday nights blacks and Italians gathered to play and dance, to heal the wounds to their hearts and minds. I was just like them, one hundred twenty years later.

I started chatting with Poggi, recalling a festival not far from Nice where I'd heard the sound of his harmonica for the first time.

Back then, I was with Ninon, a fantastic woman who happened to detest the blues. Cora didn't like the blues either. Why didn't any of my women love the music of my life?

Poggi replied that maybe the problem was me. I just wasn't capable of conveying the right emotions.

The musician had a point, but it was a matter of will. I'd always been jealous of my relationship to the blues. There were guitar solos capable of shattering my mind and body, of taking me to unimaginable levels of pleasure. A secret that I'd carry with me to the grave.

* * *

Castelgomberto, in the province of Vicenza.

The doorbell rang a few minutes early. Beniamino jerked

the door open, grabbed Fecchio by the lapel of his coat, and dragged him inside. It only took the man a few seconds to recover from his surprise but, when he tried to fight back, the pistol that Rossini pressed against his head convinced him to calm down.

The goldsmith found himself sitting on the same sofa that had accommodated the madam Cinzia Donato. He looked around and saw that there were three masked men. He didn't seem to be afraid; instead, he seemed ready to deal with this kind of situation.

He swallowed a couple of times and then asked if Marika was all right.

I reassured him. "She went to see a girlfriend."

"Then you paid her off and she sold me out," he realized, disappointed. Then his tone changed. "If you're going to shoot me, you might as well show me your face, Spezzafumo," he snapped out in dialect. "And I know your names, too," he added, pointing to the fat man and yours truly.

At that point, he sat there in silence, studying our reactions. Obviously, we remained impassive. He'd started to give us the confirmation we were looking for, and it would have been a pity to shut him up.

"That's right. Your dear friend Gastone sang like a prize canary and I recorded every word," he went on, arrogantly. "You want to kill me? Shoot me now and you'll wind up spending the rest of your lives in prison with that slut Gigliola Pescarotto, the inconsolable widow."

As he spoke he clenched his fists. He seemed ready to lunge at us. The voice, rendered hoarse by tension, seemed to emerge from the depths of a cavern.

"How did you know that you'd find gold and cash that night?" I asked.

"We'd been keeping an eye on the villa, waiting for you to organize another robbery," he replied. "When I heard that three armed robbers had knocked over a workshop in the Treviso area, I talked to the owner and asked him to tell me the details. I knew immediately that it had been you guys, and we decided to hit the villa the next night, but we weren't sure we'd find the swag. We just hoped we would."

"What we don't understand is why, once you realized that Oddo had been involved in the murder of your brother Maicol, you didn't go to the police," Max asked in a calm voice.

"Right. What turned you into a wild beast?" Rossini asked.

"The fact that my brother suffered like an animal when you shot him," he retorted, raising his voice. "It took him more than two hours to die, and he was crying the whole time. 'Kevin, help me, please,' he kept saying, and I was right there, hands and feet tied up, but I couldn't do a thing. Oddo was repaid in kind. 'Mama, mama,' that asshole kept crying."

"What about Luigina, the poor housekeeper? How much did she scream?" old Rossini asked again. "She had nothing to do with it, but you still raped and tortured her."

Fecchio shrugged his shoulders insolently. "She must have known something. And anyway, even if she wasn't in on it, she was a casualty of war. Her fucking problem that she happened to be in that house. If his wife hadn't gone out that night, there would have been three corpses."

"Four, with the little girl," I prodded him.

He waved his hands in the air. "No, not the girl. I'd have left her alone."

Turns out even Kevin had a heart.

"There's no war going on," said Beniamino. "Your brother's death has clouded your mind, or else you were born rotten and you just needed some excuse to indulge in the violence you've always liked so much."

"If you ask me, he's just a fucking sadist," said the fat man, piling on. "All that gratuitous violence just proves that he's messed up."

The goldsmith's reaction caught us off guard. "Then we're the same," he retorted, cold as ice. "Because letting a man die with a bullet in his gut is gratuitous violence. Only sickos live like parasites without working a day of their lives, robbing decent people."

He stared at us with utter contempt before going on. "But before, I wasn't like you. I'd never committed a crime. I was just a normal person: work, family, a friend or two. You were the ones who came into my place of business and threatened, and murdered, and took away everything my brother and I had sweated so hard to build.

"You don't know what work is. You have no idea of the effort, the worries we small businessmen have as we try to survive this recession.

"You're like ticks; you come and suck our blood and before you know it, you've also swept away our dreams, our hopes. You brought death into my family, and ruin. I'd lost everything; I went to get back what belonged to me.

"Not everything, of course. There are lots of things that can't be fixed. My wife and children aren't ever coming back to me, because I can never be the husband and father I once was."

He paused. He patted his linen jacket, looking for his cigarettes, and muttered that he must have left them in the car. I wanted to smoke myself, but this wasn't the right time.

"I did what I had to," the goldsmith continued. "It was my right—seeing as the government protects criminals like you instead of the citizens, does nothing but suck us dry with taxes—to make sure murderers didn't get off scot-free. And it was just as fair to save the company by taking back the gold.

"And do you guys think, after everything I've been through, that I ought to feel guilty because I kicked the shit out of Oddo's housekeeper and then fired a bullet into her head?

"You don't know it, but things have changed. People aren't

willing to take it anymore; if you dare show up to rob or steal, they want to have a chance to rub you out.

"I've been keeping an eye on you for some time now, and you've stopped knocking over workshops. But if you so much as try it, my friends and I will come riddle you with bullets fired by your own weapons, the weapons we took away from you and that we're now keeping safe, waiting for the perfect opportunity.

"I wouldn't want you to think that we're even. You'll pay, with your lives or with prison, when I decide the time is right. And the same goes for the widow."

He stared at us, his manner defiant. Kevin Fecchio had gone well beyond the thresholds of reason and common sense. He'd started down a dead-end street. This wasn't going to end well for anyone.

I pulled off my ski mask, and my friends immediately followed suit. "We don't have anything to do with Oddo, his wife, or Spezzafumo's gang," I explained, pronouncing each word carefully. "We represent the interests of Sergio Cantarutti, twelve years old, the son of Luigina, the housekeeper. She deserves justice, too, and her son deserves to be fairly compensated. That's the kind of argument you ought to be able to grasp."

The goldsmith stared at us aghast. He was so relieved that we weren't there to murder him that he allowed himself a joke. "So who are you supposed to be? The Avengers, only for the domestic help?"

"You need to think of some way to take care of this problem," Beniamino put in. "First of all, you're going to be responsible for the future of young Sergio, and then you're going to have to think long and hard about the most challenging and complicated aspect of all this: How to pay for that crime."

"What is that supposed to mean?"

"You haven't figured that out already?"

Incredulous, he burst out laughing. "Perhaps you failed to catch the meaning of everything I've been saying."

Max showed him a tiny tape recorder. "If we missed a few words, we can always play them back."

Kevin pulled his lips back, baring his teeth like a ferocious dog. "Do you think you can blackmail me with a recording? I can always say that you extorted it from me, and people will believe me because I'm Kevin Fecchio. And anyway, try to get it into your heads that I'm not afraid to die or wind up in prison because, whatever else happens, the people who hurt me will be punished. And the same goes for you."

"Do your accomplices see things the same way?" I asked. "Are you sure that Sante and Vasco are ready and willing to sacrifice themselves?"

The goldsmith leapt to his feet and started blindly throwing kicks and punches. Rossini hit him in the pit of the stomach with the barrel of his pistol, and the man found himself suddenly seated, gasping.

"Those are my two closest friends. They don't know anything about any of this," he hissed as soon as he recovered his breath. "Leave them alone."

"Then who was with you at Oddo's house?" the fat man demanded.

"Men of honor," Kevin replied proudly. "I'll never tell you their names."

The time had come for us to leave. Beniamino laid a hand on Fecchio's shoulder. "You think you've already won this match, but if you push Spezzafumo and his friends' backs up against the wall, they'll fight back, and they'll fight dirty. I wouldn't be a bit surprised if they took their vengeance out on your nearest and dearest. More blood will be spilt."

"No one is ever going to touch my family again," he snarled.

"We'll be back in touch," I announced.

"I wouldn't recommend it."

I ignored the threat. "The kid might wind up in an orphanage, even though he deserves to stay with people who love him, to attend university. It's not hard to do the math here."

Kevin cackled. "I don't even know if I'll be able to send my own kids to college, and you're asking me to pay for the education of that poor slut's bastard?"

Old Rossini gave him a slap in the face. Hard and cruel. "Her name was Luigina Cantarutti," he reminded him. "You need to learn to show her some respect, after what you did to her. The little bastard, on the other hand, is named Sergio and you owe him a lot of money."

The minute we got back in the car I called Siro Ballan and asked if his living room was available tomorrow evening. The luthier charged an extra ten percent for the short notice. "I'll vacuum the place," he snickered, convinced he was being funny. "Should I get in touch with anyone else?"

"I'll take care of it."

He took offense. "Usually I handle invitations to my own house."

"Not this time," I said, cutting him off and hanging up. Talking to Siro Ballan could be hard work.

Spezzafumo, in spite of his surprise, accepted immediately. Gigliola Pescarotto, the widow Oddo, had no intention whatsoever of attending the meeting, and I was forced to frighten her.

We went back to Padua and went out for a pizza at a place that stayed open all night. At that hour, it was deserted enough so we could speak in peace.

We were upset and by no means pleased at the way things had gone. "Kevin made it one hundred percent clear to us that he has no intention of settling the matter once and for all," I said, wiping the foam from my beer off my mustache.

"Not necessarily. He thought he was talking to Spezzafumo and his gang," Max retorted. "Now a band of strangers is in possession of a recording that screws him big-time."

"It screws everyone, without exception," Beniamino emphasized. "But I agree. The situation is no longer the same."

"If he'd wanted, he could have wiped out the Spezzafumo gang at some point in the past two years without too much trouble," I reasoned. "But maybe he was waiting for them to organize another robbery so he could kill them all and take their loot. After all, he admitted it himself when he revealed the fact that he'd been watching them."

"Fecchio thought he was talking to his murderers. To convince them not to kill him, he talked too much and was forced to play the role of the hero ready to sacrifice himself," Rossini added. "It's no doubt true in part, but we'd need to find out what his two accomplices think of it. The minute we touched that topic he totally lost it."

I sighed. "I was convinced that those boyfriends of his he's so inseparable from were the other two accomplices, but his reaction seemed sincere, at least to me."

"We'll need to uncover their identities quickly," Rossini replied. "Among other things, because we need to ascertain the different degrees of responsibility for the rapes and murder of Luigina."

In other words, we needed to figure out exactly which of them most deserved to die. One, two, or all three. I took another sip of beer and shot Max a glance. "Maybe we ought to just settle for securing Sergio's future."

The fat man just shook his head and said nothing, leaving the floor, again, to Beniamino. "You're the one who dragged us into this case," said the old bandit. "You pushed matters to the brink just to find a client, and now it's too late to turn back."

Max the Memory stretched himself out over the table. "I feel such immense pity for Luigina," he confided, his eyes glistening. "Her entire life was a rip-off, and her death was so horrible that even we pretend we don't know the details. Even in death she ended up with the short end of the stick. Someone has to pay, Marco. And they're going to."

I wasn't entirely in agreement. "The risk is that an act of justice might unleash a chain reaction."

"We can only worry about safeguarding our client's interests," Beniamino reminded me.

I nodded. And I set to eating my pizza. By the second bite I was regretting ordering one *ai quattro formaggi*—with four cheeses—because I've always found them hard to digest. But that night nothing would have been light enough for my stomach. My friends were right, that case was turning into an infernal booby trap. I didn't regret using a little sleight of hand to get the job. But I still was damn afraid that the situation might get out of hand.

That night, Cora was performing at Pico's Club. When I got there, there were only a few regulars in the audience and the sleepy pianist was trudging up and down the keyboard. My jazz woman didn't notice a thing. She shifted from one song to the next, lost in her dreams. Every so often she'd wipe the sweat off her neck with a small white hand towel. The place wasn't particularly well suited for a June night.

I was the only who clapped after a fairly daring version of *Old Devil Moon*. She blew me a kiss and was about to start in on another song when the proprietor ordered the musician to stop playing.

I caught up with her in the dressing room. "The owner wants to shut the place down for the summer," she said, disappointed.

I pointed out to her that people understandably preferred to sit outside and most clubs had made arrangements to offer that type of service.

"Not Pico's," she replied.

I smiled. "This is a club with a decidedly unusual clientele. I doubt they frequent summer bars, noisy and crowded as they are."

"And now where will they hole up?"

I threw my arms wide. "I have no idea. They'll try to survive until the fall, and then they'll come back."

Cora sighed as she began to remove her makeup. "This summer is threatening to turn into a nightmare. My husband actually wants to go to the beach in Croatia."

Every time she mentioned her spouse, I was overwhelmed with a sense of guilt. "And you're not happy about that?"

"We've always gone to Jesolo. Same apartment, same beach club, same beach umbrella," she replied. "This sudden change strikes me as an attempt to rekindle flames both in the heart and down below the belt. Not that I mind, it's just that it strikes me as demanding, when all I really want to do is relax."

I went over to her and started rubbing her shoulders. She seemed to peer up at me from the mirror as she wiped cleansing lotion over her face.

"You aren't a man I can plan for the future with, are you?" she demanded point-blank. "You don't seem like someone who could take a husband's place in terms of everyday life and general security."

"I lived with a woman once for more than two years. An ex-porn star," I told her. "She ran a bar not far from Nice. Everything was going perfectly, life was smooth as silk."

"Then why are you here with me, instead of in her arms?"

"One day I got a phone call from a friend and I left."

"And you never went back."

"No. I was just emerging from a difficult period; I was no longer the same man she'd fallen in love with."

"Do you still love her?"

"I love all the women I've ever been with," I replied.

Actually, that wasn't entirely true. One of my girlfriends, who'd gone by the name of Gina Manes, had tried to kill me, and I no longer remembered her with any special fondness.

"You're a complicated guy," she commented.

"I'm only good for a double life," I shot back, piqued.

"It's true," she admitted. "The thing is that I'd like to fall in love, let myself go, see how it turns out, you understand?"

"You have a husband and a lover who are both head over heels in love with you. If I were you, I wouldn't tempt fate."

"That was exactly what I wanted to hear," she sighed.

I'd understood perfectly. Cora needed confirmation that none of this would endanger her marriage.

She stared at me for a long minute. "What are you waiting for? Why don't you shower my throat with kisses?"

"Only your throat?"

"Do you have some other ideas?"

"A couple you might like."

"Then get busy."

"Might I suggest we take our affections elsewhere?"

"No," she replied decisively. "Any other place would make it all so squalid."

I started kissing her. Then I took her out for breakfast, even if I would have rather slept with her in a real bed, between real sheets that smelled of her perfume.

"What are you waiting for? You need to tell her the truth," Max objected when I came home. "When she finds out that you spied on her for her husband, she'll hate you forever."

"I can only love her if I omit the truth," I retorted. "It's not nice, and it's not fair, but I have no alternative."

I'd convinced myself it wasn't really all that bad. I was a discreet lover, one she saw two nights a week, no desire to be part of a real couple, just happy if the affair went on as long as possible.

* * *

We walked into Siro Ballan's living room a good hour ahead of schedule. The luthier took pains to point out that the extra time would appear on the bill. Beniamino moved the armchair he'd decided to sit in so he'd be in a dominant position should gunplay became necessary.

Usually those kinds of things weren't allowed in polite company, but murderers like Spezzafumo could hardly be considered polite.

The head of the gang of armed robbers showed up accompanied by Gastone Oddo's widow. We were certain, however, that his two enforcers, Denis and Giacomo, weren't far away.

The man understood immediately that this was no friendly visit and he became cautious when he noticed the bulge under Rossini's jacket.

Gigliola was paler than usual. "What's happened?" she demanded. "You scared me on the phone."

"And I wasn't exaggerating," I said, inviting them to take a seat. "We found out that Gastone was tortured not only to reveal the combination of the safe, but also, or perhaps chiefly, so he would tell them everything about your business. Your enemies claim that they recorded every word."

"And just who are these traitors?" Spezzafumo burst out.

"We only know one name," replied the old bandit. "Kevin Fecchio."

Nick the Goldsmith wasn't the only one who went pale. The woman blanched as well.

Then she too knew about Maicol Fecchio's murder. She was an accomplice through and through. "'For all the gold in the world, it wasn't worth it,'" I mocked her, repeating a phrase she'd repeated over and over. "That's what you said, so contritely, about the business you ran. Except that you didn't stop, not even after the murder of that poor bastard, because you don't actually give a fuck if you shoot people."

"And it was a mistake," she shot back, in a quavering voice.

Spezzafumo took a very different view of things. "This is our business."

"No," Beniamino disagreed. "And for two very good reasons. The first is that you're a bunch of dangerous dilettantes, arrogant and stupid, who take themselves for professionals, and you need to be stopped."

"What do you mean by that?" the man demanded, convinced he must have heard wrong.

"That from this moment forward, the gang is disbanded. Kevin Fecchio, by the way, is just waiting for you to put together your next job so he can wipe you out or have you thrown in the slammer for life, and we've made up our minds to keep you from acting."

"I continue to be of the opinion that you have no right to interfere," Nick stammered. He was having a hard time controlling himself.

"Once again, you're wrong," Rossini went on, "because we're in this up to our necks. We've been retained by Sergio, Luigina's son."

Spezzafumo waved the air with an irritated gesture. "Gigliola told me all about this ridiculous farce," he blurted out. "You're just using the boy to get your hands on the gold."

"That's a serious accusation," I pointed out. "But maybe you misspoke and now here's your chance to make up for it."

"I'm not interested in sitting here and letting myself be insulted by a sewer rat like you," Rossini stated clearly. "Apologize."

Spezzafumo raised his arms in a sign of surrender. "The conversation was just getting heated, I didn't mean to offend anyone."

"You'd be well advised to get as far away from here as you

can," Max broke in. "No matter how things turn out, you're fucked."

Nicola Spezzafumo poured himself a drink. "The way you tell it, we have our backs to the wall, and I don't doubt that's the case. But let me assure you, none of us is interested in running away or waiting for Kevin Fecchio to make his move, for the simple reason that we can't afford to. We have families, too, and we don't have enough money to start over again in some other country."

"And so?" I prodded him.

"Maybe it's time to find a solution that makes everyone happy," he replied, staring Beniamino right in the eyes.

He immediately understood the armed robber's line of thought. "In other words, we're supposed to help you get out of this situation unscathed."

"If you want Fecchio to compensate poor Luigina's son," Gigliola butted in, "you're still going to have to render him harmless in one way or another."

"There's one small problem you're overlooking," said Rossini. "Fecchio and his accomplices have to pay for the housekeeper's murder. Someone's going to have to die. And if it's true, as Kevin claims, that there's a recording of Gastone's confession, then there's a chance of it coming out and the cops coming after you for it."

Spezzafumo leapt to his feet. "You three are completely out of your minds," he shouted. "You think you're the law, but you're a bunch of nobodies."

"Sit down!" the widow ordered. Nick the Goldsmith obeyed without blinking. Max and I exchanged a look. The woman wasn't the supporting character we'd taken her for.

Gigliola asked me for a cigarette and took a couple of puffs and then started talking to me like a seasoned underworld kingpin at a summit meeting with other colleagues of the same rank. "Kevin Fecchio tortured and murdered my husband. If he wanted to avenge his brother's death, he should have taken it out on Nicola and his boys—the ones who actually murdered him—not on Gastone. So I have every right to retaliate against him and his confederates. But I'm willing to renounce any and all satisfaction because I believe that Lara's present and future are more important. And I'm willing to welcome Sergio into my home and raise him as if he were the son I always hoped for.

"What's more, Nicola Spezzafumo will give you his word that we'll quit the business, along with Denis and Giacomo.

"In exchange for our goodwill, you'll convince Fecchio to renounce any further action against us. After all, he's risking a life sentence, too.

"In terms of money, we can kick in with what's left from the sale of the villa and Nicola can put in thirty or forty thousand euros. More or less a hundred eighty thousand."

Silence fell over Siro Ballan's living room. The inconsolable widow had shown her true face. She'd even changed her tone of voice, her posture, her glance.

"You've been the boss the whole time," I stated, awestruck.

"But I'm not proud of that fact, not now," she confessed. "We made a mistake that destroyed our lives and dragged us right to the brink of a precipice."

"Why did you try to get us involved, through Spezzafumo, while pretending to be opposed to any further investigation?"

The woman made a face. "I simply didn't want to expose myself the way I was forced to do today," she explained. "It's been two years of pure hell, lived in grief, apprehension, and regret. Gastone wanted to shut down operations entirely after Maicol Fecchio's murder. I was opposed, and I had my way. Gold is cursed."

Bullshit. That woman was a pretty skillful manipulator; her technique was to feign sincere regret for her mistakes. I'd fallen for it before but now her words just left me cold.

I had only one last, overriding question. "Did you mean it when you said you wanted to take care of Sergio?"

"So, are you interested in the proposal?"

I shook my head in disappointment. "I just wanted to understand whether for once a shred of truth had passed your lips or if it was just part of your usual playacting."

"I'm not acting, I'm just trying to survive."

Nick the Goldsmith started to get impatient. "Well then, what have you decided?"

Max stubbornly insisted on seeing his bluff. "We only care about the kid. It'll be the way events play out that'll decree your fate."

It was the widow who showed her cards. "I don't understand why you're being so stubborn," she said. "It's obvious that if something happens to us, something'll happen to you, too."

We acted surprised. "What do you mean?"

"If they arrest us we'll do our best to stave off a life sentence without parole by tossing them anything that can give us bargaining power; of course we'll give them your names. It's news to nobody that law enforcement has been interested in putting Signor Rossini behind bars for years now.

"But if Fecchio wants to seek out justice himself and causes us any harm, we're going to consider you responsible."

"That sounds very much like a threat," I told my friends.

"Heavens," the fat man added. "I would never have expected it, but we're dealing with two eminently respectable criminal minds here."

Beniamino was in no mood for irony. "We've done you the considerable courtesy of apprising you of the situation, even though we had no obligation to do so, since you're not our clients. In the course of this meeting, you've insulted us and threatened us.

"In accordance with our rules, right now I should pull out

my gun and make you swallow every word you just uttered. But we're good-hearted people and we're going to give you a second chance; because we brought you bad news today, you got scared, and all the bullshit you just spouted is the product of ill-advised improvisation. So we invite you to think carefully, because we're not going to give you a third chance."

"Improvisation only makes sense in jazz," I muttered for no particular reason. Maybe because I'd have rather spent that time with Cora, instead of sitting in Siro Ballan's living room.

Spezzafumo and the widow left and we sat in silence, thinking, smoking cigarettes and sipping little glasses of liquor.

Civilians often have no idea that the inner workings of the underworld are so twisted that criminals turn to violence because it may be the only way to find a simple solution. Especially for minds like that of Nick the Goldsmith. Gigliola Pescarotto herself was hardly a genius, though she was certainly more clever than he was. It couldn't have been complicated for her to put together that gang and dominate that group of men. The problem was that the losers would drag the winners down into ruin with them. It was all apparently so absurd, but there actually was a sense to the logic that had led to the clash between those two gangs of armed robbers, albeit a horrendously perverse one.

Greed and contempt for human life on the one hand, and on the other a deranged and exaggerated idea of justice and property. An explosive blend, and we'd just relit the fuse.

"Maybe it wouldn't have been a terrible idea to get rid of Spezzafumo," Max muttered.

Old Rossini ran his hand over his forehead. "The worst idea imaginable, if you ask me, though it's no good hoping that Spezzafumo is just going to go away. He's one of those losers who survive because they're not afraid of going to prison and they think they're too clever to be killed. A soldier. It's no accident that he gets his marching orders from that witch, the widow Oddo."

"What are we going to do?" I asked.

"What we've been talking about doing for quite some time now: hunt down Fecchio's accomplices," Beniamino replied. "We need to know all the pieces on the board if we want to figure out if there's a solution."

"What if we don't find one?"

"We'll board the *Sylvie* and leave the party. And every month we'll send a little money to the boy."

Right. We were the only ones with nothing to lose. And we were the only ones who would keep our word, whatever the cost, and look after Sergio. Someone needed to come out the other end of that horrible mess.

Tracking down Kevin's mysterious partners wasn't going to be easy. These were people with no connections to the underworld, without criminal records. To join the goldsmith in that undertaking meant that they'd been through the same things. An armed robbery, one of their family members murdered. They felt sure they were on the side of the angels and they'd be an endless source of problems, right up to the very end.

PART TWO

A farmer noticed the car parked, one of its doors open, by the side of a canal and gave the alarm. The fire department scuba team took a couple of hours to find the corpse tangled in the vegetation on the bottom.

The news of Kevin Fecchio's death flooded the entire region. All the media outlets discussed it, especially the many local TV broadcasters who almost immediately subscribed to the theory of a suicide. The portrait that was offered to local public opinion was that of a healthy country boy with solid Venetian roots who had been devastated by a twist of fate and found himself struggling beneath the weight of a terrible tragedy.

The thing that drove him to it was identified as the total lack of justice for the murder of Maicol. No one had been arrested, tried, and sentenced. And Kevin, who had fought so hard for the rights of citizens to self-defense, hadn't been able to contain the grief and regret that had devoured him.

The local journalists didn't mince words when it came to the authorities or to his wife, who was guilty of having abandoned him, and depriving him of his children's love. They called her a whore, and there was no appealing that judgment.

The autopsy revealed nothing out of the ordinary that might point to other theories. The considerable quantity of alcohol found in his stomach had no scientific explanation but journalists and columnists had no doubt that it had helped him screw up the necessary courage.

102 · MASSIMO CARLOTTO

We were the only ones who were convinced that Kevin Fecchio hadn't intentionally thrown himself into that miserable little river. Truth be told, Nicola Spezzafumo must have shared our views because he hurried to see us, swearing that he'd had nothing to do with it and announcing he'd be suddenly heading off on an overseas vacation.

A multitude of citizens attended the funeral. The church, which had stated, through the person of the bishop, that there could be no doubt that the dearly departed had been the victim of a tragic accident, had organized a service befitting a prominent member of the community.

A gigantic lie had become an official truth with all the blessings.

We'd blended in with the mourners and were studying the faces of the men in search of the slightest clue that might point us in the right direction. I worked my way into the knot of law-and-order proponents, now orphaned of one of their most outspoken leaders, and listened to muttered comments that proved worthless.

A cathartic burst of applause greeted the coffin when it emerged into the open air.

"I don't want to see anyone clapping their hands at my funeral," Max muttered.

"They won't," I reassured him. "You've made your wishes clear."

Each of knew the last wishes of the others, since there was no way to know in advance the order of departure. They faithfully reflected what and who we were, and they all had in common the absence of a service of any kind, and cremation. To tiptoe off the stage as light as cinders. In part because there's nothing worse than a half-deserted graveside.

The crowd began to scatter and the bars started filling up. It was almost noon and most of the orders were for white wine or spritzes.

Max asked the waiter to mix equal parts Aperol and Campari for his spritz. The man nodded, his grimace that of someone who's heard it all in his lifetime and thinks that just one more can't make things any worse.

Beniamino ordered a fine Sauvignon. "I'm sick and tired of this ritual of the spritz," he said. "Frankly, it doesn't seem good enough to go crazy over."

Max was in agreement. "There's better, no doubt. And really, we ought to go back to the classic 'ombra' of wine or else to more serious aperitifs, in terms of alcohol, too."

Rossini pointed at the fat man's glass. "Then why do you drink it?"

"It's another lost battle and I've just decided to fit in," he replied, his voice serious. "That way, I have something in common with all these nice people."

The old bandit looked at me. "When he starts theorizing about even the stupidest things, I can't stand him."

"He just can't bring himself to admit that he can't live without it," I explained. "The same thing happens to me, anyway. It's cool, it's light, and I don't care if it's fashionable."

"You'll never take me alive," Beniamino reiterated.

We'd have gone on discussing this relevant, crucial topic for a good long time if we hadn't been distracted by a fight that broke out among a group of customers. Sante Zanella, Kevin's childhood friend, was ready to rearrange the facial features of a compatriot who had suggested that the deceased had been "a bit of drunk."

Many others intervened to calm things down, and we took advantage of the opportunity to observe Sante from up close. We'd already ruled him out as an accomplice in the Oddo home invasion, but he was one of the two people closest to Fecchio, and it was hard to believe that he was entirely in the dark.

The other man apologized, trotting out the old theory that

any Venetian is liable to have one drink too many in his own defense. And it was then that Sante supplied us with a very interesting piece of information: The "misfortune" had occurred on a Wednesday. Kevin, however, liked to drink a glass or two on Friday and Saturday night, since he wouldn't have to go in to work the next morning. He would never, ever allow his employees to see him working off a hangover. That was one of Maicol's rules and he would never have betrayed his brother's memory.

And to Sante, this was proof that his friend's death was a suicide, the suicide note that Kevin hadn't managed to write.

The others all fell silent and at that moment I would have loved to tell them that actually, the abundance of alcohol in Fecchio's stomach was proof that he'd been murdered by his accomplices. The very same people with whom he'd planned and carried out a home invasion that involved grand larceny and, worse, double homicide.

Kevin Fecchio was radioactive, and they'd decided he was too risky to keep around.

His partners had rid themselves of him in clever, elegant fashion after learning that three thugs had laid an ambush for him in the home of a prostitute and that he had blabbed indiscriminately because he'd been positive he'd been dealing with the Spezzafumo gang.

It had become necessary to murder him to burn all bridges linking them back to their crimes, to keep anyone from being able to trace their real identities.

From the very beginning we'd been betting that the notorious recording of Oddo's confession, whether or not it actually existed, wouldn't surface.

Fecchio's murderers had no interest in bringing the cops into the matter. The case would have drawn so much attention that the minister of the interior himself would have been bound to provide men and resources to bring them to justice.

A case that seemed destined to explode, taking with it everyone connected to it, had been defused with a simple murder. Everything had been hushed up and both Kevin's accomplices and the widow Oddo could count on getting off scot-free.

But we couldn't toe the party line. Our client hadn't obtained satisfaction of any kind and as far as we were concerned the investigation continued.

Beniamino went back to Punta Sabbioni and to his jaunts aboard the *Sylvie*. He had no interest in suffering the brutal heat that had been forecast for some time, and which was now slowly roasting the Po Valley. Padua was like a flaming match and the old bandit abandoned us to our fate, a prolonged and complex phase of the investigation: scouring old news records for any case that might have something in common with the crime that had first changed Kevin Fecchio's life and figuring out whether any of the victims had ever subsequently crossed paths with him.

We were convinced that to forge an understanding strong enough to form a gang, they couldn't live very far apart. They must have spent time together and become intimate, a path punctuated by a long series of encounters steeped in hatred, resentment, and bitterness. Their grief over the things they'd suffered had sent them straight to hell, and they'd made up their minds to stay there.

So we started to focus on the most savage crimes perpetrated in the province of Vicenza.

Max looked up from the folder of newspaper clippings he was perusing. "The first time I seriously considered seeking revenge was when they killed my Marielita."

I felt, as I always did, a stabbing pain in my chest. For me too that was a particularly painful memory. She'd died in my arms, hit by a burst of bullets fired by the local mafia that had dominated Veneto back then—at least until the clan's capo,

Tristano Castelli, sold his gang out to the state like some bankrupt corporation.

"And the death of her murderers actually made me feel better," he added after a brief pause.

"Revenge always provides a healthy dose of satisfaction and comfort, even though its limitations are unmistakable since it's incapable of restoring to you that which has been taken," I commented with considerable conviction. "And in any case, it must be an act of justice. The exact opposite of the barbarity of Fecchio and company."

"I still don't really understand why they acted like butchers in a splatter flick. If they'd limited themselves to murdering Spezzafumo and taking back the gold, no one would have really objected."

I slapped my chest. "Because they don't have outlaw hearts," I shot back. "If civilians decide to go beyond the bounds of their laws, they lose all sense of proportion. Even when all they're doing is embezzling public funds. They turn into sharks, they become predators."

"It's not that simple, Marco."

"I think it is. Those three let themselves go and commit truly vile acts because they were convinced they had the right to do so. They went into that villa certain they'd be absolved of their sins because they were sure their victims were guilty, and as such deserving of nothing but contempt."

"And once we got involved, Kevin was sacrificed because he was endangering the impunity of the two others."

"A preemptive murder," I pointed out. "These people weren't born yesterday."

"And I'm pretty sure they'll have other surprises in store for us," the fat man added, going back to his reading.

Between the Internet and Max's archives we managed to reconstruct a bloody map of armed robberies carried out against villas, goldsmiths' workshops, and jewelry shops.

Organized crime had given up the tradition of robbing banks in grand style and had focused in on private citizens, who were less able to defend themselves.

Terror and brutal violence. The Oddo home invasion numbered among the cruelest in a long list of tragedies. And for the cops it was never easy to track down the culprits. The Northeast of Italy was a borderland and the gangs attacked and then retreated with the greatest of ease.

The contempt for human life displayed by this new brand of globalized crime sent shivers down the collective spine. For that matter, it was perfectly in line with the attitudes that now dominated the world. And there wasn't the slightest indication that things were going to improve.

On the third day we identified a possible candidate. It was Sunday and in Greece the people were about to vote in a referendum that would decide their economic future. The rest of Europe applauded this pretense of democracy at gunpoint.

The man we were looking for might very well prove to be a certain Ferdinando Patanè, age fifty-four. He'd come up from southern Italy at the end of the seventies and opened a jewelry shop in the center of Dolo, one of the most prominent towns along the Riviera del Brenta.

In the winter of 2009 two distinguished gentlemen with "Slavic" accents entered and pulled out their guns. Patanè's son, Lorenzo, age twenty-one, a promising engineering student at the university of Padua, was in the rear of the shop. The robbers shot him in the back while he was facing the wall because, according to their unappealable judgment, the father had been too slow to provide certain answers.

The young man survived, miraculously, but was left paralyzed from the neck down. His mother Geraldina had told the story of the family's tragedy with great courage and dignity. She tracked down local journalists and pushed them to keep the public informed about her boy, who no longer had a future.

Patanè, the father, on the other hand, had been reluctant to talk. It seems that he was torn by a sense of guilt at not having been able to reach the handgun he kept in a drawer. He'd shut down his business without fanfare and devoted himself to his son. Rumors circulated in town: that the jewelry shop was insured for a ridiculously small sum and that the merchandise that had been stolen was worth a large fortune. Mistakes you pay for.

Maicol and Kevin Fecchio were among the very few who had come to express their solidarity, a moment immortalized by a photographer at the front entrance of the hospital where Lorenzo had been taken. Patanè was a loyal client of theirs, as the two brothers had explained to the reporters, and "the tribulations they were experiencing constituted an endless injustice that could be blamed on a state that had long ago given up its responsibility to protect merchants and business-men, allowing criminal gangs from eastern Europe to ride roughshod over the territory."

The statement had clearly been tweaked by the author of the article but the concept was clear.

The jeweler had repaid the courtesy by attending Maicol Fecchio's funeral. The two men must have cultivated a pretty solid friendship because Patanè had locked arms with Kevin.

After the service, Patanè, recognized by the journalists, had given a series of very short statements all of the same tenor: death penalty, right to self-defense, absent and impotent government.

We'd found pictures and reports of their friendship up until a couple of months prior to the robbery in the Oddo villa. Then nothing. The ex-jeweler hadn't showed up at Kevin Fecchio's funeral, and he'd probably produced some credible excuse, since nobody had commented on his absence.

Instinct and experience told us that we'd tracked down one of Kevin's accomplices. But there was a very persuasive argument that he'd had nothing to do with the torture and the murders. Kevin was a strong man, in tip-top shape, perfectly capable of slipping a ski mask over his head and carrying out a violent crime, while Ferdinando Patanè was short, skinny, and frail-looking. He certainly wasn't a man of action and we could safely rule out the idea that he'd set foot in the villa. Up until then, our theory had been that the group was made up of three men. But if Patanè was a part of the conspiracy, as we suspected he was, then it meant that there was a fourth man. At least.

An unlicensed investigator like yours truly could hardly turn to the police for information. Unlike my officially registered counterparts, I had to steer clear of the cops, who could only bring trouble.

In twenty years of work as an investigator I'd managed to sidestep the issue by constructing an extensive network of informants in the densest underbrush of Venetian society. All of them people who were frequently living archives, or else capable of laying their hands on solid information on short notice.

Prominent among them was the category of con men. The Veneto boasted a long and venerable tradition in the art of pulling a fast one. Once Max had shown me a long list of local companies that produced a disparate array of goods, in particular in the electromedical field, all of them regularly denounced by consumer unions. The miraculous devices they made were actually worthless frauds, but dazzling TV commercials convinced hundreds of naïve consumers to sign disastrous contracts, put together by certain unprincipled Paduan law firms.

Mirko Zanca, my informant in the Dolo area, was a well-respected professional con man. We'd met him when he was passing himself off as a follower of Dr. Ryke Geerd Hamer and his Germanic New Medicine. He'd opened three offices in as many provinces and he treated patients who'd lost faith in traditional medicine with natural pharmaceuticals of his own invention, foisting off on them that old fairy tale about the correlation between unhappiness and pathologies.

He wasn't particularly expensive; he charged between eighty and a hundred euros because he felt this was his mission. The truth, however, was altogether different: Zanca felt no pity and he was indifferent to the suffering and death of the people he was pretending to care for.

That was a distinctive characteristic of the category: cold indifference to one's fellow man. Con men ruin anyone they can get their claws into. Including their relatives. I'd known quite a few and over time I'd become convinced that this was a crime that should be subject to serious investigation by the psychiatric community, not just sanction by the criminal code.

We had been hired by the wife of a cancer patient; she was exasperated by her spouse's decision to stop his radiation therapy because "Doctor" Mirko's treatments were undoubtedly more effective.

We'd talked to the oncologist who was treating him, and he'd confirmed that it was absolutely necessary for the patient to return to his treatment at the hospital.

The next day we showed up at Zanca's place without calling ahead, and old Rossini, after leveling a gun at his head, explained that he'd have been perfectly happy to pull the trigger, but that his friends here had asked him to refrain. He personally didn't see the reason. As far as he was concerned, people who deceived and defrauded the sick needed to be shot.

"Don't kill me," the fake physician had shrieked in terror. "I swear I'll disappear. You'll never hear another word about me."

And he'd kept his promise. He'd saved his life but he hadn't eluded the long arm of the law. The sudden closure of all of his clinics had aroused the suspicion of several patients who'd reported him to the police. He'd been convicted of aggravated fraud and passing himself off as a licensed physician and sent to prison.

After he got out he recycled himself as the All-Knowing Mirko, an expert practitioner of white, red, and black magic, capable of solving problems of love, sex, and work.

The All-Knowing Mirko received every day by appointment, in a small apartment not far from the center of Dolo. He turned pale when he recognized us, but the absence of Beniamino reassured him to the point of becoming particularly talkative in his attempt to justify himself.

"I'm not doing anything wrong," Zanca started out. "I tell people what they want to hear, that's all. And I swear on my life that I never accept the sick as clients. If they have so much as a hangnail, I send them home without asking for a cent. As you know very well, sick people cost me a fright that nearly gave me a heart attack—what with that friend of yours—to say nothing of the three years in prison."

"Satisfy a curiosity for me," the fat man interrupted him. "Say an out-of-work man comes in here, so desperate that he decides to turn to a seer to find work; how much time and money does he have to squander before finding out that you're just a piece of shit?"

"Actually I am a psychic," he pointed out, by no means offended. "And really, the ones who come to see me are for the most part the mothers, the girlfriends, and the wives. Let's say that a complete evaluation of the case can run to about three hundred euros. But I don't go any further than that because all I do is remove the evil eye that bars the way to good fortune. That good fortune may then choose to show itself or remain concealed. None of that depends on my magic."

Max looked at me. "Are you hearing this?"

I shrugged. "Our man Mirko will never change. In any case, we didn't come here to talk about his powers as some fucking wizard. We're here to get some information. If he chooses not to provide us with what we need, then we'll have to call our friend, the nasty one."

"I know everyone in town," he blurted out, jovial and enthusiastic. "I'll be delighted to be of assistance."

"The Patanè family," I said under my breath.

The con man's face darkened. "All I can give you is gossip," he muttered. "People used to talk about them more, when the tragic story of what happened to the boy was on everyone's lips, but now they lead a quiet life, see very few people; they haven't even been seen in church in quite a while."

Max reached out a hand for one of my cigarettes. The psychic made a face, probably even considered for a moment the idea of asking us not to smoke, but then understood that that wouldn't be a very good idea.

"How are their finances?"

"People around here say that for a few years they were really struggling," replied Zanca. "The parents were forced to go around looking for money more or less everywhere. Now, though, things are going better. I've heard other rumors to the effect that a few anonymous donors gave them the money they needed for medical care and support."

Well, just think of that. It would be dangerous to try to reconstruct the timeline of those unhoped-for donations with a sewer rat like this psychic, but I was pretty sure they'd come sometime after the home invasion in Oddo's villa.

Max put his cigarette out on the corner of the desk, which looked expensive. Zanca turned his gaze away.

"Anything else to report?"

"A specific question might be helpful," the con artist pointed out, impatient to see the last of us.

"We'd like to know who Patanè sees. His closest friends, of course."

Zanca raised his arms in a gesture of surrender. "I don't know and I don't even know who I'd ask," he said. "I often run into Signor Ferdinando pushing his son's wheelchair, but they're always alone."

It was almost dinnertime by the time we left the psychic's offices but the heat hadn't dropped by so much as a degree. We took a table at a bar just a stone's throw from the state highway, jammed with cars crawling along no faster than pedestrians.

"I hate him," Max burst out suddenly, referring to the con man. "I'm telling you, it was all I could do to keep from wrapping my hands around his throat."

I took the straw out of the glass. I hated to suck on my aperitifs. "He's just one of many," I objected. "The world is full of them, and he's not even one of the more dangerous ones. Compared to the people who sell adulterated food or peddle counterfeit pharmaceuticals, our Mirko looks more or less like a dilettante. The only thing he has in common with those others is his unmitigated gall."

The fat man changed his tack. "Why on earth are we spouting such obvious platitudes?"

"Because we're chasing our tails around a case that's only going to give us a bunch of headaches and pains in the ass if it turns out Patanè is involved."

Max sighed and stalled for time by sipping his spritz. "Even if he's the guiltiest one of all, he's still untouchable."

"That's exactly right. The day his parents die, Lorenzo will experience the tragedy of a life dependent on care provided by strangers, but until then, he'll rely on their presence."

"The boy's needs take precedence over everything else," the fat man said.

"We'll have to be very cagy in how we convince him that

he's earned his impunity, otherwise he'll have no incentive to betray his accomplices."

We weren't a bit happy to find ourselves in such a complicated situation, one that forced us to accept choices that were hard to live with. Max immediately made it clear how annoying he found it.

When I paid the check and left a more generous tip than usual for the waitress, my friend found immediate fault.

"You did it just because she's cute," he objected.

"Very cute," I emphasized.

"That strikes me as rude and sexist."

"You're right, but I don't give a flying fuck."

"Don't you see how wrong it is to behave this way?"

I saw red. "We're sitting here splitting hairs, trying to decide whether or not to gun someone down in cold blood, and you decide to bust my balls over this bullshit?"

He fell silent for a few seconds while he mulled over a response. "The fact is, I ought to have realized long ago that your political immaturity has always prevented you from acting, in your daily life, with decency," he got out all in one breath. "That's why I think it best if I withdraw my critique and treat you to a compensatory dinner. Seafood, of course. I know a couple of restaurants around here that are to die for."

I burst out laughing and slapped him on the back. I knew how much I annoyed him.

We spent the following day trying to track down Rossini and come up with a rough strategy to flush Patanè out and obtain the evidence we needed.

A complete waste of time on both counts: Beniamino must have been at sea or hiding away in some inlet along the Dalmatian coast, and putting the ex-jeweler of Dolo's back to the wall would require a brilliant idea that continued to elude our collective minds.

I left home around midnight and headed to Pico's.

Cora dedicated *All Day, All Night* to me, a song that was a hit for Carmen Lundy in 2001. During a break, while the jazz woman went to redo her makeup, the piano player told me there was something wrong with the way she was singing. An inexplicable tension that was weighing down all her songs.

"I hadn't noticed," I said.

"Of course not. All you think about is screwing her in that smelly dressing room."

"Watch your language."

"You don't fucking get it; if this keeps up, sooner or later she'll go to pieces. You know what happens to an old 78 rpm record if you drop it? The same thing'll happen to her."

I stared at him in surprise. "You're jealous. No doubt you're right about her; you know the business, you're an insider, but clearly you like her."

He ran a hand over his head with a slow gesture. "What with all the time we spend together, she's gotten under my skin," he said, and then he headed off to the bar.

I'd have liked to talk to Cora about her jazz stylings, but the minute I shut the door behind me she slid her tongue into my mouth and undid my belt.

Between a kiss and a glance, she slipped her hand into my briefs and started brushing my balls with her fingernails.

"Does that work?" she asked.

"Very nicely."

Then her hands took charge of my cock, caressing it.

"Stop," I implored her.

"No."

"I'm begging you."

"No."

Later, at the usual café, I talked to her about the piano player's concerns, without letting her know that the man had a crush on her. That was none of my business, plus I was sure that she'd already noticed.

"I'm searching for the 'center' of my jazz," she snapped, irritated. "I need to range freely, to delve deeper in my performance."

I was tempted to tell her that she was spouting bullshit like a fire hose, but I zipped my lips. That lasted just a few seconds. "What's wrong?"

She shrugged. "Nothing."

She finished her brioche and added: "It wasn't a decision not to have children."

"What does that have to do with it?"

"I don't know, I was just saying. I wanted you to know."

"Okay. I thank you for telling me," I said brusquely.

"But it doesn't mean a damn thing to you."

"No. Nor do I feel like I have a right to know the reason why."

"Right, you're the lover."

"That's exactly right," I retorted. "Are you looking for a fight, Cora? In that case, I should let you know I'm not at all good at that kind of thing."

"What's that mean?"

"I'm too slow for snappy answers," I explained. "The right thing to say occurs to me ten minutes too late."

She burst out laughing. But slowly. The faint creases I liked so much began to smooth out and then take shape again, one after the other, without the slightest urgency.

"Go home and get some rest, tired jazz woman," I whispered.

While I was waiting for the elevator, Signorina Suello, our favorite neighbor, caught up with me.

"You guys didn't come to the condo board meeting," she said, a slight note of reproof in her voice.

"And we never will come, either," I confided.

"Are you and your friend homosexuals?" she asked, point-blank.

"That's our business, don't you think?"

"Forgive me, it's just that everyone in the building is convinced of it. Do you want to know what they call you?"

"I'm not interested, thanks."

"No matter what they say, you two are the most likable tenants here as far as I'm concerned."

I thanked her and pulled out my keys. When I walked into the living room, I found Beniamino in red-and-white striped boxers reading the paper. He was in a bad mood, too. "You've peppered me with phone calls and texts and forced me to come running back to this oven of a city," he grumbled. "I just hope there's a good reason."

"Where's Max?" I asked, lowering the temperature of the air conditioning by a degree.

"In the shower, and anyway it won't change a thing."

"What won't?"

"Fooling around with that remote. There's only so much cool air you can coax out of that gadget."

I went into the kitchen to make myself an espresso and discovered that the fat man had purchased another espresso machine, one that guaranteed coffee as good as what you'd get at a café. Only I didn't know how to work it, of course.

I resigned myself: after all, pots and pans and gas flames were his domain and messing around in that devil's playground was no more than his right. I settled for a glass of cold milk that left an unmistakable stain on my whiskers. I'd been neglecting my mustache and it had thickened into an untidy mess. I discarded the idea of going to the barber. It was too hot out to let anyone wrap a towel around my neck.

Max, as part of his complete life-overhaul project, had decided to use a new cologne and he insisted on asking us to sniff it on his skin.

My opinion was neutral, while Rossini was definitely against it. "It doesn't suit you," he decreed. "You need to veer toward patchouli-based scents. They're more appropriate for you fatties. They make you more likable."

The fat man took offense. "Are you serious?"

"No," Beniamino replied tersely. "But you've been harassing me with this damn smell that I don't give a shit about, while what I want is to be out on the open water."

At last we found we were concentrated enough to take on the challenge of investigating Ferdinando Patanè. Only in movies and on TV are investigators actually capable of tailing people even in small towns.

In Dolo we'd be found out in less than half a day. There was no point in even talking about tapping phone lines or installing ambient listening devices in his car or living room. I'd have known whom to hire, but in that situation it made no sense. The former jeweler needed to be confronted face-to-face and forced to collaborate if he was guilty, and if not, our most sincere apologies.

"Have you found out anything new?" asked Rossini.

"Right now, Patanè is the only clue we have to follow," I replied.

"If it turns out to be unfounded, then we're really in trouble," Max explained. "The premises and the research method are doubtless valid, but they're time-intensive and require lots of checking."

"If you ask me, he's involved," I said, feigning confidence. "There's a picture showing Fecchio and Patanè together. They're looking at each other as if they're shaking hands to seal a pact. As if they're sharing something important. Do you know what I mean?"

"Yes, and now it's also clear which of us will go have a chat with this guy," said old Rossini.

I didn't object for the simple reason that I couldn't wait.

The heat forced father and son to put off their usual walk

till a little later. Ever since Lorenzo had come home from the hospital, Ferdinando Patanè had chosen the best time of day to push the wheelchair along a route that included both banks of the Naviglio del Brenta. In fall and winter, around midday, or even earlier if the sun was out; in the spring, in early afternoon; and in the summer a few hours later.

The previous day, we'd followed them from a distance, to ascertain their route and to choose the place in which to confront them. We'd settled on a bridge. I was planning to deliver my whole appeal in the time it took to cross it, little more than a minute. In sixty seconds, you can say a lot of things. TV taught us that lesson many years ago. The problem was how to start. It's an art practiced by call-center sales teams. If you get those first words wrong, you've lost the customer for good.

They left the building a little after 7:30 that evening. The mother accompanied them to the front gate. The building was so square, white, and nondescript that it looked as if it had been drawn by a child.

I waited for them at the agreed-upon spot. Lorenzo was wearing a light-blue baseball cap over his thinning hair and wan face. He was looking straight ahead, his gaze grim but lucid. His father never stopped talking. From his facial expression, I guessed he was telling him a funny story.

At the right moment, I came up beside them. The ex-jeweler, alarmed, swiveled his head around fast.

"Fecchio's death was a brilliant move, but it actually served no purpose," I started off nonchalantly. "If you want to stay out of jail or the grave and go on pushing this wheelchair till the day you die, you're going to have to betray someone, Signor Patanè. Everyone, actually."

The man stared at me, terrified, and went on walking like a robot.

"Stop, Papa," Lorenzo ordered. With a tip of his head, he motioned me over until I was standing in front of him.

"I know you have a tape recorder in your pocket," he continued. "But still, I want to be clear: You can go fuck yourself, you and all your friends, who I'm guessing are somewhere nearby."

Surprise overwhelmed me. "Do you think you can bullshit your way out of this situation?" I ventured, more or less at random.

A sarcastic smile appeared on his face. "Do what you have to," he hissed.

"Lorenzo, please," Patanè whined.

I took advantage of the opportunity to play the family card. "Don't you ever think about your parents?"

"They're a constant feature of every endless day and you'd only be doing me a favor if you got rid of them," he grinned. "The day of the robbery my mother forced me to go down to the store to clean up the workshop when all I wanted to do was stay home and study. And my dad managed to get me shot. Instead of grabbing that fucking pistol and risking life and limb to defend his son and the shop, he started sniveling, exactly as he's doing now, and he couldn't even remember the combination to the safe in time."

I turned to look at Ferdinando Patanè. He was gripping the wheelchair to keep from collapsing. He was a little man, broken by grief and remorse. It had to be a terrible thing, facing his son's implacable hatred day after day, but I didn't pity either of them. They were still accomplices to horrible crimes.

I changed strategy. "As you know very well, since we informed Kevin Fecchio of the fact, we represent the son of the housekeeper who was murdered along with Gastone Oddo."

"I don't know what you're talking about," Lorenzo interrupted me. "Though of course if it's the way you say it is, that kid may be running some risks himself."

I ignored the threat. Young Patanè's objective was clearly to make me lose my temper.

"We're going to stay on you until we obtain the names of your accomplices, the ones who took part in the slaughter," I said, my words clear and my tone harsh.

"I continue to have no idea what you're talking about," the son retorted sarcastically. "But if you're done harassing us, I'm afraid I need to head home so my mama can change my big-boy diaper."

The father turned the wheelchair around and started pushing. His back curved, his gait hesitant.

Kevin and Lorenzo: white-hot hatred. Pure, lethal. The idea of punishing and robbing criminals had sprung from their meeting, ripening in minds clouded by hate.

Ferdinando: a good-natured shopkeeper, a weak man whose sense of guilt had turned him into an accomplice.

The other two showed up later and were given the task of aiding in the assault on Oddo's villa, along with Fecchio. They couldn't have been selected purely on the merits of their determination to punish criminals with their bare hands. It was certainly a necessary condition, but not in and of itself sufficient. The two accomplices would have to be possessed of specific operational skills and a particular propensity for violence. Not everyone's capable of transforming himself into an armed robber, a rapist, and a murderer on the spot.

Lorenzo had won the first round. He'd gotten rid of us, and for a while we wouldn't go back to bother him. The way he'd slammed the door in my face still stung. For being just twenty-seven, he had a way with words. But it wasn't just that. I'd taken the pair's respective roles for granted because he was in a wheelchair. A stupid preconception.

After the crushing blow of our failure with the Patanès, we'd gone off to lick our wounds aboard the *Sylvie*. Beniamino had organized a light repast with an array of delicacies, chief among them Stilton and Sauternes. While we were nursing our wounded egos by stuffing our faces, we'd started going over the case, detail by detail; it was, as the fat man had rightly pointed out, nothing more than a series of fucking Russian nesting dolls.

Late that night, while I treated myself to a generous helping of calvados before stretching out on my bunk to try to get a couple of hours of sleep, Beniamino said: "In this case, we've committed one error of judgment after another. Let's try not to forget who we are and where we come from."

Then he raised his glass. "To Marius Jacob, and to all free men with outlaw hearts." Max and I joined in the toast.

The Marseillais criminal Marius Jacob had been the inspiration for the literary character Arsène Lupin. An artist of theft and a dedicated old-school libertarian and anarchist, at the turn of the twentieth century he'd robbed the rich to help fund utopian movements and help the needy. Once, he broke into the home of a physician by accident, and not only did he refrain from taking a single thing, he even left a note of apology. His targets were society's parasites. France rid itself of him by loading Jacob onto a ship bound for Cayenne and a life of forced labor. He shuffled off this mortal coil in 1954, leaving a suicide note and two liters of wine for whoever found his body.

The history of European crime over the past century and a half included the lives and exploits of a great number of gentlemen bandits. Their experience over time had resulted in the construction of a code of behavior to which we scrupulously adhered.

Thieves, smugglers, armed robbers, men and women who rebelled against the logic of organized crime and the various mafias, in perennial conflict with the corrupt. A practically unknown history, but one that we were proud to be part of. A history of people on the losing side, women and men who had lived through their eras with their heads held high and their dignity intact.

I set the empty glass on the table. "It isn't easy this time," I said, before getting up and wishing them goodnight.

* * *

Dolo. Office of the All-Knowing Mirko.

The con man took fright when he recognized Rossini. "What have I done wrong this time?" he stammered.

"Calm down, Zanca," I said. "We just want to ask you a few more questions; not about Ferdinando, about Lorenzo Patanè."

The con man pulled anxiously at his chin while peeking over at Beniamino. He had the look of someone who's put his foot in it.

"What is it?" I asked, my voice hard.

"The conversation we had three days ago got me thinking and I reached out to a few of my customers, asked some questions," the man replied without taking his eyes off the old bandit.

"We told you to keep your mouth shut," Max reminded him.

"Maybe I can be useful to you," the psychic lied.

"Maybe you could get a little money out of it," I shot back. "You couldn't resist the temptation to worm your way into the Patanè household to sell your magic skills, am I right?"

"I thought they might be of some comfort."

"And I continue to think that you ought to die, to rid humanity at large of your noxious presence," said Rossini, who was examining the amulets scattered around the room.

"I might have found the person who can supply the information you're looking for," sniveled the con man.

"And who would that be?"

"A nurse who quit last year. From what I understand, she couldn't take young Patanè's bullying anymore."

"Are you able to get in touch with her?"

"I have her cell phone number."

"Call her and tell her to come here."

The psychic fished a scrap of paper off a tray, picked up the phone, and put on a show of his ability to deceive others. "She'll come at 3 this afternoon. She can't make it any earlier," he informed us, wiping the sweat off his neck.

To kill time while we waited, we purchased swimsuits, beach towels, and flip-flops, and took refuge in the nearest public pool. We weren't the only ones to have had that magnificent idea; children and their mothers made their presences known by screaming, often for no reason.

I took care not to complain to my friends, because experience had already taught me how that would turn out. Old Rossini would berate me, accusing me of acting like the usual radical-chic elitist who claims to love the people while detesting their behavior.

At that moment, Beniamino was enjoying a pleasant conversation with two Ukrainian nannies off from work, while Max was on his tablet, searching the Internet for news.

"The Senate commission on justice is playing its usual games to prevent torture from being included as a crime in the penal code," the fat man informed me indignantly.

I shrugged. "That proposal's never going to pass and even if it were to, it'd be so watered down that they wouldn't be able to prosecute anyone."

"It's worth giving it a try," Max retorted decisively. "The list of cases and deaths is getting longer and longer."

Every so often the fat man would talk about civil and human rights in terms a self-righteous civilian might employ, forgetting how well he actually knew the reality, which was that our armor-plated democracy saw torture as just another resource. The justifications and the apologies always came much later, long after that resource had been fully exploited.

That the cops had carte blanche to lock down the streets and extort information was strategic to the government's long-term plans. Though of course no one was supposed to overdo it or, most importantly, get caught red-handed.

The criminal proceedings that laboriously worked their way through the system before emerging into a courtroom were turned into obscene puppet theaters. The victims were attacked and derided by a well-oiled media machine capable of harvesting consensus from the majority of public opinion.

The few who raised their voices in opposition were the usual intellectuals, artists, and professors who could afford to. And in any case they always counted for less and less. People are generally willing to renounce the rights of others if it means living in peace and tranquility.

Nothing new, for that matter. Public safety, investigations, the very administration of justice, prison—all institutions based on violence. Physical and psychological violence. Threats and blackmail were common practices.

Many years ago, I'd gone with Max to an excruciatingly dull public panel discussion on the Mafia. I had however been impressed by the pitiless realism of a Palermitan Jesuit who had maintained that suspicion was the prelude to truth.

And in fact, priests have the long tradition of the Inquisition behind them. In the end, the method hadn't changed; it had simply been refined and adapted to modern times and requirements.

Rarely did the discovery of the truth occur without the use of at least one of the countless forms of violence.

We knew that very well. We'd adjusted to it without the slightest moral qualm because throughout the history of the underworld, there had never been any ambiguities. And even in the case at hand, approached, as it was, with criminal intent by everyone involved, there was no room for doubts and hypocrisies.

Nor was there on our part. Our outlaw hearts, however, recognized a fundamental difference: Torture and rape weren't part of how we operated. Quite the opposite.

To investigate means asking questions and obtaining truthful replies. Whatever the cost.

"This is stunning!" Max blurted out, interrupting my chain of thought. "The new mayor of Venice has banned forty-nine children's textbooks because they call into question the traditional family. He's afraid that the gay lobby is trying to corrupt children's minds."

The first citizen of one of the most beautiful cities on earth was an industrialist. He'd promised prosperity and had trounced his opponent: a judge who had instead promised respect for the laws, and had never had a serious chance of winning. The city of Venice was coining cash money as fast as it could shuttle tourists through. The problem was whether to give the whole city entirely over to business interests or make some attempt to protect it from unbridled invasion. The citizenry had made its choice.

I got up from the lounge chair. I needed something to drink. "And you're worried that in the Senate they're not sufficiently sensitive to the issue of torture?"

"I worry about everything, Marco," Max replied, his tone ambiguous.

I slaked my thirst with a couple of glasses of white wine, went back to lie down, and decided to catch up on some sleep. I dreamt of a woman from my past who'd suddenly reappeared and wanted to marry me. If it had really happened, I would have thrown myself at her feet.

"The sun isn't kidding around," Max exclaimed in a serious tone a few hours later, as we were walking toward the psychic's place of business. "The greenhouse effect and the hole in the ozone have made the sun potentially quite dangerous and it's important to protect oneself."

"Who are you trying to palm that sermon off on?" I asked.

"You," he replied seraphically. "Beniamino doesn't need sunscreen because he got a tan out on the water, but you're white as a sheet and you forgot to put any on, and now you're red as an overripe tomato."

I lowered the car's sun visor and studied myself in the mirror. The fat man was right. I ran my hand over the back of my neck and felt that it was tender to the touch. "I really did get burned. I need some kind of lotion or I'll go through hell tonight."

Max handed me a small tube. "It's a good thing I went to the drugstore and stocked up."

"You're certainly careful about your health aren't you?" Rossini needled him.

"If it's the diet you're referring to, I'd like to point out that I haven't put on so much as a gram of weight," the fat man said by way of excuse, snickering with gusto. "I'm preserving my fat as if it were a UNESCO World Heritage site."

When Zanca ushered the nurse into the room set aside for consultations and magical rituals, we found ourselves face-to-face with a very attractive woman in her early forties. Nice face, long legs. The only things that clashed were her hair, cropped short, the beige, raw-linen skirt suit in a cut long out of style, and her sandals. They were identical to the ones an old high school teacher of mine used to wear.

Rossini was sitting in the armchair, Max and I on either side of the desk. An image straight out of a TV jury: the latest round of assholes examining the competitors, who try to persuade them that they have the necessary expertise and skills.

"Have a seat," Beniamino began, pointing her to a chair a couple of yards away.

All-Knowing Mirko squeezed her arm. "Listen to these gentlemen, Serenella, they have an interesting proposal to make you," he said, before leaving as he'd been told.

She obeyed with docility, but the expression on her face suggested something else entirely. She didn't understand what was happening and our presence was making her uncomfortable. "Who are you and what do you want?"

"Journalists, cops, insurance examiners, circus performers," I replied. "Whatever you're thinking is fine because it doesn't matter. What does matter, though, is the fact that we're willing to give you cash in exchange for certain information about Lorenzo Patanè."

Serenella was a pragmatic woman. "What kind of information?"

"We want to know who he saw when you were taking care of him."

"And how much are you offering?"

Rossini pulled a wad of bills out of the breast pocket of his jacket. "Five hundred."

"Two thousand," the woman countered.

We pretended to discuss this amongst ourselves. "All right," said Beniamino.

"And five free sessions with All-Knowing Mirko."

Max took advantage of the opportunity to have some fun. "If the information is first-rate, we'll give you ten."

The nurse nodded in satisfaction, pocketed the cash, and started telling what she knew.

"At first the house was always full of people, then it slowly emptied out. Lorenzo never accepted what had happened to him and as time went on he became increasingly unpleasant. I was forced to leave because he tormented me with questions of a highly personal nature, he wanted me to tell him about my private life, and when I refused to do so, he would get cruel. He was unbearably insulting. I later heard that they hired a male nurse but that he's not happy either."

She wasn't telling us what we wanted to know, and I politely pointed that out to her. She went straight to the point.

"While I worked in that house, I occasionally saw Kevin Fecchio, the businessman who killed himself recently, and Vick Bellomo, Lorenzo's best friend. He came to visit quite often when he was in Italy. But I saw them only when I had to work late, otherwise I wasn't there by the time they arrived. But I knew they'd been there because of the stink of cigarettes and the dirty glasses."

"Did Bellomo leave the country frequently?"

"Yes, he'd stay away for months at a time, but now he's stopped. About two years ago he opened a pub nearby, in partnership with another guy who worked with him."

"And what line of business was he in?"

"From what I was able to gather from the conversations between the Patanès, he was a policeman of some kind and worked as a bodyguard for some very important men."

"Same as his partner in the pub?" I asked.

"So I heard."

We exchanged satisfied glances. Those two guys had all the marks of men with a past as military contractors, mercenaries who worked security in war zones. Five thousand euros a month and a license to kill. Very little was said about the Italians who went to work in these companies whose profits boggled the mind. Very little indeed. Italians are, after all, good people.

Signora Serenella left satisfied. She hadn't had to say anything compromising and she'd earned a nice wad of cash, to say nothing of the comforting power of the All-Knowing Mirko's magic, though Mirko came close to fainting when he discovered that he'd have to defraud the woman free of charge.

"That's not fair," he objected. "Ten sessions are too many."

"Get used to it."

"You don't understand. Serenella has romantic problems, she's divorced and she wants to get back together with her husband, who's started seeing another woman in the meantime, a much younger woman, obviously."

"So?"

"These are matters you can settle in two, three sessions at the most because there *is* no solution. If I drag it on for so much longer, it means that I really have no powers, and Serenella will go around telling everyone just that."

Beniamino put a hand on his shoulder. "You have our heartfelt sympathy."

The psychic was surprised at the old gangster's jovial tone, which was due solely to the fact that for the first time we could risk a bit of optimism.

Max turned on his tablet and did a few Internet searches. "Bad Boys Pub," he read out, "owned by Ludovico Bellomo and Salvatore Adinolfi."

A few seconds later, we were admiring their pictures on the bar's Facebook page. They were big and strong, gym-hardened, their heads shaved and their sideburns dense and sculpted. If it hadn't been for the difference between their complexions and a few of their facial features, they could easily have been taken for brothers. Ludovico, "Vick," was young, he must have been twenty-seven, perhaps twenty-eight, the same age as Lorenzo Patanè. Adinolfi was somewhere between thirty-five and thirty-eight.

"Maybe we've reached the last of the Russian nesting dolls," I said.

"We'll collect a little information and tomorrow night we'll go have a beer at these gentlemen's place of business," Rossini proposed.

We never did set foot in the Bad Boys Pub. In twenty years of work as an investigator I'd never found myself forced to consider atmospheric events among the variables of a criminal case. And it hadn't been since 1930 that such a destructive tornado had touched down on Italian soil. Just a few hours after our meeting with the nurse, the Dolo district was devastated by the fury of a cyclone packing winds of more than 185 miles per hour. Nothing was left of one venerable old villa but photographs to testify to its one-time existence and beauty. The roofs were torn off hundreds of homes; pieces of furniture flew into the air as if they were sheets of paper.

Volunteers, journalists, and politicians looking to gather votes converged in great numbers. The situation was far more serious than it had at first seemed.

A small item in a local paper told us that the Patanè home had also been seriously damaged. Apparently the Bad Boys Pub had fared even worse. The proprietors had spread the word that the place would be closed for the next month.

Old Rossini decided to go see for himself and discovered that the roof and part of the kitchen had been damaged. A couple of weeks, no more, the contractor in charge of the repair work had guaranteed. A likable, talkative young man, who envied Vick and Salvatore because they'd taken advantage of the situation to go on vacation.

"They're on the move," Beniamino announced when I answered the phone. "They've decided to beat us to the punch."

PART THREE

S cattered across the belowdecks table on the *Sylvie* were disassembled weapons that Rossini was cleaning and oiling with meticulous care. "They took advantage of the tornado to disappear," I said, trying to piece together what had happened, "but I can't believe that they've already figured out who we are and are ready to kill us."

"You forget that Fecchio wasn't the first one who had dealings with us. They've had all the time they needed to investigate," Max objected.

"What do they know for sure?" Rossini asked.

"That we represent the housekeeper's son," I replied. "We told that to both Kevin and the Patanès."

"And then everything they wrung out of Gastone Oddo," added Max the Memory.

"Their most likely targets then could be the little boy, the widow, and the Spezzafumo gang," Beniamino summed up, pushing a gun brush through the barrel of a .45-caliber pistol.

"Sergio is twelve years old, doesn't know a thing, and I doubt they're planning to hit him to get at us. It would be a senseless move," I retorted. "Now that we've identified Lorenzo Patanè, they feel vulnerable, and it's logical to assume they're planning a bloodbath to protect themselves."

"I agree," said Beniamino. "We need to alert that harpy, Gigliola."

"I'll take care of it," I said.

"And I'll take care of gathering information about the two

ex-contractors," Max added. "I know a journalist who's been monitoring local recruitment for quite some time."

"Okay. I'll go look in on the boy, just in case we've got it wrong," Rossini concluded.

While I was driving toward Piove di Sacco in my beloved Škoda Felicia, listening to Papadon Washington sing *The Blues Is My Story*, the volume on full blast, I received a phone call from Cora's husband.

"She has another one, now I'm sure of it," he complained.

I was sure of it myself and, relieved to hear that he still hadn't figured out it was yours truly, I feigned a detached and professional stance. "And how did you find out?"

He said nothing, uncertain whether or not to answer the question. "The laundry hamper," he muttered.

"Excuse me?"

"I opened the hamper to drop in a shirt and a whiff of the smell of 'man sex' filled my nostrils."

This wasn't the first time I'd run into spouses who'd discovered an affair thanks to a particularly well-developed and suspicious sense of smell.

"That's all?" I replied at random. "It doesn't strike me as reliable evidence."

"Listen, I don't want to come off like an obsessive husband who gets to the point where he's sniffing his wife's panties, but I don't want to be taken for a fucking idiot either. I need to know what's going on here."

"I understand. So what are you planning to do?"

"It must be someone who hangs out at that club where she sings."

"And so?"

"I want to go there in person. I need the name, and the last time we talked you forgot to give it to me."

It hadn't been an oversight. "If I were you, I wouldn't show up while she's singing. She'd never forgive you."

"What the fuck do you know about it? You weren't even able to figure out that she was sleeping with another man."

"You don't know that."

"Let me be the judge of that. What's the name of that damn place?"

I heaved a sigh. "Pico's Club."

"I'm glad you gave me back that retainer," he said in a combative tone. "That way I don't have to ask you to give me my money back."

He hung up before I could retort. I was tempted to call the jazz woman and warn her, but I couldn't do it for the simple reason that she was convinced that I didn't know her husband.

A fucked-up situation. All I could do was wait and hope that in the inevitable clash between husband and wife, my name didn't come up.

The gray roots at the center of her scalp were so unmistakable that for an instant I was tempted to point them out to her. But I decided against it the instant I remembered who I was dealing with. That detail too was part of the character that Gigliola Pescarotto was playing: the woman overwhelmed by a cruel and relentless fate, now surviving on her own strength alone.

"I'm surprised by this visit," she said in a bored voice. "I thought that, with Kevin Fecchio's suicide, the whole case had been closed once and for all."

"You forget that we have a client."

"Cut it out with that bullshit, tell me what you want and get the fuck out of my hair."

I liked her better as a gang boss. "Don't be rude, I just came here as a gesture of courtesy, I could have spared myself the effort."

"And maybe that would have been better."

I lost it. And I really let her have it. "The only reason I'm here is for your daughter, to keep her from coming to a bad end."

She changed her tune. "What's going on?"

"We've identified the rest of the gang that killed your husband and poor Luigina. They thought they were safe after killing Kevin but we've managed to track them down."

"Who are they? Give me the names of those animals."

That day everyone seemed to be demanding information from yours truly. I shook my forefinger sharply. "No," I told her, and I couldn't help but mock her. "Not even for all the gold in the world."

"I have the right to know."

"You forget that I have no obligation toward you whatsoever," I retorted. "What I can tell you is that right now they're at large, armed and dangerous. They definitely have something in mind, maybe they're planning to come pay you a visit, or rub out the Spezzafumo gang."

She grabbed her sewing shears. "Tell me who they are. Otherwise, how the fuck am I supposed to defend myself?"

"Don't threaten me," I hissed. "See if Nicola and his henchmen can protect you, though I'm pretty sure the other guys are stronger. One good piece of advice is to take your vacation early this year."

She lost her temper, lunged to her feet, and tried to run me through with those shears. Luckily she was skinny as a nail and after a brief struggle I managed to disarm her and knock her to the floor with one shove.

"Pack your bags and run," I repeated to her as I left the office.

Her shouts followed me out. "But where? For how long? You're just going to get us killed, you bastard."

I stopped at a nearby bar. I was shaken. That hand armed with sharp steel trying to find a way to tear open my chest had scared me. I ordered an espresso and a grappa.

A few minutes later, Nick the Goldsmith called. "We need to meet."

"We don't have anything to talk about."

"You're putting us in a dangerous situation that will only create problems. Problems between us, too."

I was tired of being threatened by despicable creatures. "You didn't even deserve the warning you got. We behaved properly and there are certain things you have no right to bring up."

Spezzafumo was no fool. He realized he'd gotten off on the wrong foot. "We could join forces," he proposed.

"We wouldn't so much as have a cup of coffee with you guys, so forget about forging an alliance."

"It would be in everybody's interest."

"True," I agreed. "But we don't want to have anything to do with people like you."

"You're insulting me."

"I'm glad to see you get my point."

I heard him sigh. "You're shutting off all room for negotiation."

"That only ever existed in your imagination."

"There will be consequences."

"At this point, I'm going to have to remind you of what Rossini said about your threats and ask you to back the fuck up. You know how it works."

"Don't make me laugh. There are three of you, but the old man is the only one who counts for anything. You and the fatso are only good at blowing hot air. Either you give me all the information you have about those guys this very second or you'll pay for it dearly."

I hung up and ordered another grappa. Nicola Spezzafumo was a poor idiot and there was no way to fix the mess he'd just made.

I went back to Padua. I found Max standing in line at an ice cream shop not far from home. He didn't know what flavor to get and it was impossible to get him to listen to me until he'd chosen between three types of vanilla and four types of chocolate.

Then he ate the ice cream in a hurry, chomping the cone down as well, to keep the heat from turning it to slush.

After an espresso and a cigarette, he declared himself ready to listen to me. "Be patient," he said, excusing himself. "But sometimes, if I don't satisfy my nervous hunger, I can't think straight."

Now I was suspicious: "What's happened?"

"The journalist, you know the one who reports on contractors?"

"She didn't give you the information."

"No, she turned out to be very cute and very helpful."

I immediately guessed what had happened. "So cute that you tried something and she sent you scurrying."

My friend had an afflicted expression. "She said straight out that she didn't like obese people, whether male or female. She believes that excess fat is a symptom of slovenliness and weakness."

"So what did you do?"

"I thanked her for the favor and left with my tail between my legs."

"You didn't say anything back? She was needlessly nasty."

Max sighed. "I know, but then and there she laid me out; it was as if she'd kicked me right in the balls. Luckily, in the freezer I found the usual pan of eggplant parmesan made by that sainted woman, Signorina Suello."

"At least four generous portions."

He put his arm around me. "Exactly. And then the ice cream, the espresso, the cigarette, and now when I get home I'll have a shot of something strong to help digest it all, and I'll be ready to examine our case without being distracted by my wounded ego."

"But she was cute, at least?"

"Yes, she has an ass that, in spite of everything, continues to enjoy my most boundless admiration."

Ludovico "Vick" Bellomo and Salvatore Adinolfi had met in Libya where they worked as bodyguards, protecting Italian businessmen for a Belgian company. They came from different backgrounds. Bellomo had served briefly in Afghanistan as well, while Adinolfi had spent a couple of years in Iraq.

They weren't well-known individuals and they'd never traveled in ideological circles. They seemed to be interested in just one thing: money. In fact, they'd both been fired without notice because, according to the woman Max got his information from, the two of them had attempted to loot one of their clients' houses.

"Fucking mercenaries, in other words," I commented.

"If it hadn't been for them, Fecchio and Patanè would never have had the nerve to organize that home invasion."

I, in turn, I brought my partner up-to-date on my friendly conversations with Gigliola Pescarotto and Nicola Spezzafumo.

"The woman tried to bump you off and the other one threatened you for the third time," the fat man commented. "You know what's going to happen when Beniamino hears about it. The rules are clear; the widow will be spared because she has a little girl, but Spezzafumo is a dead man."

"I know," I said. "And since that's an indisputable fact in this mess—because you can't leave someone alive if he might decide without warning to pump you full of lead or else hire someone else to do it for him—let me suggest a potential solution to the case, factoring in that grim probability."

The thought had occurred to me while I sat nursing my

second grappa at the bar where I'd received Nick the Goldsmith's phone call.

The parties at odds had always reasoned per very specific criminal viewpoints, and it mattered little that a couple of civilians like Fecchio and Patanè, who claimed motives nobler than filthy lucre, were involved. To put an end to the feud, it was necessary to remain within the context of that twisted criminal logic.

In the underworld, when situations arise that threaten to end in a bloodbath, the thing to do, if possible, is arrange for negotiations that will at least limit the number of corpses. My plan called only for Spezzafumo's death, while Gigliola, Denis, and Giacomo could retire to private life, which, after all, is what they had already been ordered to do.

Now it was necessary to limit the damage on the other side, and the only way to do that was to create the conditions that would allow for dialogue. Unlike what most people might imagine, when rival gangs have a serious problem to resolve, they talk early and often before moving on to the mass slaughter option.

It didn't take much effort to talk Max into it, and I called Rossini, who was standing sentinel, guarding the boy's safety. "How's it going?" I asked.

"No sign of anyone."

"I'd like to go back and have a chat with the father and son, but I need you to approve it."

"Can you tell me anything more?"

"No."

"What does Max say?"

"He's in agreement."

"Then so am I. Do your best to come back in one piece."

The Patanès' house had had its roof ripped off by the tornado. Huge plastic tarps covered the roof, now stripped of its terra-cotta tiles, until the construction workers could tend to it.

A neighbor told me that they'd moved to a small house made available by the township of Dolo. It wasn't far away and it only took me a few minutes to find it. A small yard and a single-story building designed for the handicapped. As I approached the privet hedge surrounding the yard, I peeked into the kitchen where Signora Patanè was making dinner. I walked all the way around the house, but it seemed that the woman was alone just then.

I guessed that the father and son were out on their usual walk, and I waited for them, sitting in my car, continuing the therapy advised by Catfish with a piece of "contaminated blues" by the Funky Butt Brass Band.

I checked my cell phone for texts from Cora. Though I had my hands full with a situation that meant beginning to draw up a list of the soon-to-be dead, the jazz woman was still always on my mind. I wanted to see her, love her, wrap her in my arms and kiss her.

I was hopelessly in love. But I'd never uttered a word to convey that concept to her clearly. I was afraid I'd chase her away. She'd always been careful not to let slip a single word that would violate the code to which illicit lovers adhered. Strictly by the book, even though I was certain she liked me, a lot, and that she thought about me and desired me in return.

But we were both well aware that I had nothing to offer her. I was the lover she'd say goodbye to someday.

I pushed the off button on the stereo when I saw the wheelchair emerge from a narrow side street.

Father and son were walking in silence, faces strained with tension. Between their damaged home and the two former mercenaries on the run, they must not have been feeling very comfortable.

I got out of the car and headed toward them, putting on a nonchalance that I did not, in fact, possess.

As soon as Ferdinando saw me, he stopped pushing the

wheelchair. They were both staring at me, with different expressions. Fear and contempt.

Lorenzo was a tough nut. He was convinced he had nothing to lose and maybe that was true.

"You should hear me out," I said, showing them I wasn't hiding a recording device. "We want to give you a chance to find a way out."

"Why such a magnanimous gesture?" the young man snickered.

"To limit the number of deaths and the general fallout from a gang war," I explained, as if I were a broker explaining to a customer why it's in his interest to invest in the stock of a given company. "Bellomo and Adinolfi can eliminate some of your enemies, but then what are they going to do? Go back to pulling draft beers until someone walks into the Bad Boys Pub and rubs them out?"

I leveled my forefinger straight at Lorenzo, who seemed to have been seriously stunned by the fact that I knew the names of his accomplices. "You don't give a fuck about your parents. You've made that clear, but after them it'll be your turn. And you're wrong if you think they won't find a horrible way to make you die. There was an Albanian, once, a guy just like you, who acted like a smartass because he was convinced he had nothing to lose. He was a big enough asshole to besmirch the memory of a local boss's father. You know what they did to him? They locked him in a cellar full of starving rats. They heard him scream for days."

Ferdinando Patanè gave in to the tension and sat down on the edge of a low wall. "I always said it would end badly," he stammered in a broken voice.

"Shut up!" his son ordered. "I can't stand you when you act like this."

"You have no chance of getting out alive," I insisted. "The time has come to talk and find a solution."

"Which would be?" Lorenzo finally made up his mind to ask, announcing a de facto surrender.

"Bellomo and Adinolfi, along with with Kevin Fecchio, raped, tortured, and murdered Luigina Cantarutti. One of the two must die," I replied in a flat voice. "And after that, you have to compensate Sergio, Luigina's son, by paying him three hundred thousand euros."

I was pretty sure that they weren't in possession of such a huge sum, but this wasn't the time to haggle.

The two of them stared at me as if I were crazy. Ferdinando's jaw actually dropped.

"What you're asking is impossible," Lorenzo muttered. Fear was finally forcing him to think.

"Not a bit," I retorted. "You just need to take one more step down the ladder of criminal degradation, and so far you've shown yourself more than able to do that."

"Perhaps we should confess everything to the carabinieri," the father broke in; he was clearly having trouble breathing.

"It's a respectable option," I acknowledged. "We don't like it because we'd lose the money earmarked for young Sergio, but it would certainly help to prevent future bloodshed. And it would result in the trial of the century, with the spotlight on your son, the criminal mastermind, who planned home invasions and brutal murders and was ready and willing to betray a man as popular as Kevin Fecchio. Your lawyer will certainly have a hard time trying to talk the court out of sending him to a penitentiary clinic where he'll spend the rest of his life sucking other convicts' dicks."

Ferdinando Patanè burst into tears. His son did have a point: The old man was a real crybaby. I handed him a piece of paper with a cell phone number jotted down on it.

"We want a meeting with Bellomo and Adinolfi, too," I said. "You'll have to be present. Call me when you're ready."

"You really have no pity!" the father sobbed in anger.

"Pity died with Luigina," I reminded him. "In these kinds of situations, there's never room for friendly feeling. You've shown you can think like low-ranking Mafiosi. Keep that up and you'll be fine."

I turned on my heels and left, abandoning the two of them to a grim despair they'd never be able to shake.

As for me, though, I was more than satisfied. Lorenzo had immediately given up all brash trash-talking, proof that the two ex-mercenaries were by no means capable of resolving the situation. They'd have to hide out somewhere while they tried to figure out what to do next.

And then there was a chance we could wrap up the whole mess, I'm not going to say discreetly, as we'd hoped, but at least without attracting attention from cops and reporters, who certainly had better things to do than to dig into a case they would have all much preferred to leave unexamined.

In prison, in order to survive and to keep the place from becoming even more unlivable, I'd invented a job as peacemaker among the various underworld factions. A hard, challenging, dangerous calling, but one that taught me to understand mindsets and behaviors and, above all, to understand that the more a door seemed to be locked, the harder you needed to keep on knocking.

For that reason, after briefly informing my partners as to my plans, I headed for Piove di Sacco to resume discussions with Gigliola Pescarotto.

At that time of night the knitwear plant was closed and I studied the GPS map to find the best way to approach her house without risking surprises. I was positive she'd ignored my advice to leave town for a while.

I parked two streets away and cautiously ventured closer, hugging the hedges in front of the yards. The dogs caught my scent immediately, but I wasn't too worried. In the summer dogs bark for no reason at all and the owners usually aren't too alarmed. The widow's house was shrouded in darkness, and here and there a few shafts of light filtered out through the closed roller shutters. I stood there, watching from the shelter of a tree. After ten or so minutes, I noticed the blaze of a lighter and then the dot of a cigarette ember that glowed red with every puff.

It had to be either Giacomo or Denis. Probably one was staying inside while the other one hid in the darkness outside. So the widow had chosen to wage war. She'd spirited her daughter to safety and now she was waiting for the butchers who had murdered her husband. It wasn't an intelligent strategy—assuming of course that she hadn't devised some other diabolical twist.

I went back to my car and called her.

"That wasn't very nice of you, trying to kill me the other day," I said.

"Don't exaggerate. I just wanted to do a little embroidery work on your face to convince you to be more cooperative."

"Horseshit. You lost control," I shot back. "Anyway, I assumed you were on the Riviera and instead you're barricaded in your home with a gorilla standing guard that even a blind man wouldn't miss."

She remained silent for ten seconds or so, the time it took her to understand I wasn't far away. "Where are you?"

"Nearby, if that's what you're asking, but it never crossed my mind to come pay a call on you," I replied. "For now I'm happy just to talk. Nicola Spezzafumo could be a subject we both find interesting."

"And why would that be?"

"Yesterday he crossed the line. And he's never stepping back over it."

"That's what you say."

"You know that's how things are going to go."

"So what if they do?"

"Well then, we might be able to make a deal. Either you and his orphans devote yourselves to honest, hardworking lives here in the homeland, or else you emigrate to the Americas like Venetians in the nineteenth century, and every last reason we might have to bicker will be forgotten."

More silence. Longer this time. "It seems to me like an offer to be taken into consideration."

I closed my eyes to concentrate on every single word. "Then we can talk it over," I confirmed.

"Of course we can! The sooner we end this mess, the better it is for everyone."

"Nick is an old friend of yours," I countered.

"And I'll remember him fondly for as long as I live," said Gigliola.

She was lying. I was sure of it. By now she was an open book. After Kevin Fecchio's murder, she'd understood that she could start the gang back up, continue with the old plan to pull off a few more jobs, and then leave the country. And flourish somewhere else. Tear off the mask of a grieving widow and become what she'd always dreamed of.

With Nicola Spezzafumo in place of Gastone Oddo. Probably they were already planning a robbery, no matter how clear old Rossini had been when he'd warned them not to keep any of their criminal activities up.

With her and Spezzafumo, there was no room for negotiation, but taking it to the bitter end would mean a defeat for everyone. For the living and for the dead. I was sure she'd done her math and double-checked it; I was also confident she'd taken into account the fact that our rules prohibited sending a mother whose daughter had no father into a premature grave, even if that mother was a criminal of Gigliola Pescarotto's caliber.

The unwritten laws that guided the world of illegal activities were complicated and difficult to interpret. They were part of a world on the verge of extinction, a world to which we stubbornly belonged. The globalization of organized crime that represented the onset of modernity had eliminated all these laws. The only regulatory bonds guiding organizations now were relationships of force. We were among the few free men still scrupulously observing the rules. It was the only way to protect the weak, the victims. Along with our consciences.

I went back to Padua and dropped by Pico's. This wasn't the right evening to see Cora but I wanted to have a chat with the piano player. When the jazz woman was off, he played in a trio with a guitarist and a clarinetist.

I waited for the first intermission to intercept him at the bar.

"Can I get you something?"

He glared at me. "He's the one you ought to treat to a drink," he replied, pointing at the barman who nodded with a smile.

"Okay, but do you mind if I ask why?"

"Last night, Cora's husband handed me ten euros to tell him if there was anyone buzzing around her," he snickered while he made a gin and tonic.

My blood ran cold. "And what did you tell him?"

"That I didn't know a thing. For ten euros I'm not getting my hands dirty, but for fifty . . ."

I pulled out my wallet and slapped two fifty-euro bills down on the table. "One of these is for you and the other one covers the musicians' tabs."

He made them disappear with all the skill of a prestidigitator.

"Then what did the husband do?" I asked.

"Nothing. He listened and left before the show was over."

"Did she see him?"

"I'll say she did! I've never seen her so pissed off."

And once they both got back home, there would have been

a screaming fight. I felt sorry for Cora. She didn't want her husband to discover her island of freedom but I couldn't keep the secret; it would only have made him more suspicious. "What a fucking mess," I thought to myself, as I decided to stay on and drink another couple of glasses.

I got home slightly tipsy and was introduced to Antun and Dalibor, two taciturn Dalmatians that old Rossini had called in, just in case we ended up needing to use our guns. They were both more or less Beniamino's age, and they looked so menacing that I decided not to ask them any questions about their pasts. In the former Yugoslavia, organized crime hadn't remained neutral and on more than one occasion had played a decisive role in operations of ethnic cleansing.

"Rossini is coming back," Max informed me. "There's absolutely no one anywhere near the boy."

I gestured to our guests with a nod. "We have our own mercenaries," I whispered.

"You're wrong," the fat man retorted. "They're here out of friendship. Rossini is godfather to their grandchildren, but that doesn't mean they're not 'lethal killing machines.' That's how our friend described them."

"I'm going to bed," I announced. To help me fall asleep, I searched for an especially soporific channel. I concentrated on a televised sale of toiletry products for senior citizens. I collapsed without even getting up to turn off the TV.

We all have our own little obsessions, our harmless idiosyncrasies that, with the years, become routine. I, for instance, quickly tire of any given shaving cream. After a couple of months I toss it out because I can't stand it anymore. An appointment, every morning, with the same blend of scents, the same consistency of foam, annoys me and, at the same time, makes me suspect that the shaving cream in question isn't of the highest quality or, in any, case isn't well suited to my skin.

And so I bade farewell to a Portuguese shaving cream beloved of barbers all over the world since the turn of the twentieth century, tossing the tube into the trash.

I decided that very same morning to visit a popular perfumery in the center of town where a shopgirl, a particularly cute one, by the way, had no difficulty talking me into purchasing expensive niche products that, to judge from their packaging, looked more like old leftovers from some warehouse.

The kitchen table was set as if for a wedding feast, certainly not for breakfast. Beniamino's two friends had brought a number of bottles of plum grappa, as well as sheep's milk cheeses.

I tossed back a couple of shots before dipping a croissant into my *caffè latte*. During my second cigarette, smoked in blessed peace, absorbed in the reading of one of the many daily papers purchased by the fat man, the cell phone rang. The one whose number only the Patanès knew.

"Hello?"

"We agree to a meeting," Ferdinando stammered.

"At ten o'clock tonight on the banks of the canal where poor Kevin 'committed suicide.' You know the place well."

I went back to the kitchen, where Max was holding forth on the Greek situation, which still dominated the front page of all the newspapers. "Tonight we have the Patanès," I announced.

"Good!" Beniamino exclaimed. "Finally something's starting to move. But in the meanwhile, we have to make sure we don't lose track of Spezzafumo."

"I'll take care of it," I said and went to get dressed. Before going out I pulled a couple of rolls of cash out of a hiding place built into a credenza by some clever carpenter. There were a couple more hiding places scattered around the apartment. We only used cash. We had no bank accounts, and we were completely unfamiliar with credit and debit cards. Leaving traces of your cash transactions was dangerous for individuals who have 'no visible means of support,' as was printed clearly on our files, still preserved in the archives at police headquarters.

First, I went to see my favorite salesclerk in the shaving section. She broke all the old records by convincing me to buy the entire toiletries line put out by an English house that I'd never heard of before. But she was unable to talk me into the eau de toilette that brought out the fragrance of the aftershave lotion. I'd been using the same eau de toilette for years. It had first been given to me by a woman I'd never forgotten and it carried the name of the sword of the Ottoman knights. Over time, I'd learned to distinguish the top notes from the middle and base notes, and when you're that in tune with a scent, you must never make the mistake of switching to another.

Carrying an elegant paper sack with the shop's logo, I went to a tall building on the outskirts of the downtown. On the sixth floor were the offices of an insurance company. The secretary knew me by sight and wrongly believed I was a client. Between a smile and a flurry of comments on the new heat wave, which the weathermen had dubbed Charon, she ushered me into a claustrophobic waiting room where I leafed through financial planning magazines.

Twenty or so minutes later, I was shown to the office of the big boss. He called himself, quite prosaically Mario Bianchi—an extremely common name—but he was actually a prince of the Venetian underworld. The façade was that of an eminently respectable insurance executive, but the business that had made him rich was that of clandestine investigation. Once or twice, I'd worked for him. He had resources, professionals, and covers at his disposal. And he would stop at nothing. He was rotten to the core, but if you were part of the underworld, you could count on a certain degree of discretion. He'd treated me well because he knew that as long as I was protected by Beniamino Rossini, I remained untouchable.

Neither short nor tall, roly-poly, horn-rimmed glasses, and an unfailingly optimistic expression stamped on his face.

"What do you need?" he asked.

"I need four subjects checked out," I replied, handing him the list of names and the address of the Pescarotto residence. "One woman and three men. She travels between her home and a small business. Just now, she's being protected by the three men; they take turns. I suspect that they're in the middle of planning a criminal act, a robbery. A few days. I'll inform you once I no longer need the coverage."

He nodded. "You know the fee."

I pulled a twelve-thousand-euro retainer out of my pocket and set it down on the desk. At fifteen hundred euros per person, that was equivalent to two days of surveillance. Mario Bianchi commanded a high fee, but in case Spezzafumo went to meet his maker, no one would be able to connect my interest in his person with that murder.

I decided to stay out. An aperitif in the piazzas, lunch at Anfora da Alberto, and then to a multiplex to watch a couple of movies. Why the movie theaters tended to run B-grade horror movies during the summer would forever remain a mystery to me.

I watched two of them just to kill an afternoon in a dark, semi-deserted theater with good air conditioning, but the plots were flabby and contrived.

I turned up at cocktail hour. Max had set the fixings up at home, with delicacies meant to please Antun and Dalibor's palates.

At a certain point Rossini got up. "It's time."

We arrived at the rendezvous in two cars a good half hour ahead of time. The Patanès and the two ex-mercenaries were already there. Ferdinando was standing behind Lorenzo's wheelchair. Bellomo and Adinolfi played their roles to perfection. They got out of an SUV garbed and armed as if they were expecting a firefight with a platoon of terrorists. All for show. I'd been right when I'd decided that the mercenaries were low-level lackeys. I peered over at the two Dalmatians. They were snickering, unimpressed, the barrels of their assault rifles pointing at the ground. Rossini was holding his pump-action shotgun like a boar hunter would. His eyes were focused on the hands of the two assholes. At the first suspicious move, he'd send a hail of pellets blasting in their direction.

I took a few steps closer, illuminated by the headlights of the cars. I was about twenty yards away from their weapons.

"I'm happy that you've accepted this meeting," I said, speaking loud enough to make myself heard. "In these situations, talking is always a necessary step in the process of finding a solution. I hope you also appreciate the choice of location. We suggested it to make you understand that so far every decision you've made has been a mistake. Including the decision to eliminate Kevin Fecchio. You were such good friends and yet you didn't hesitate to lure him out here and drown him. I'll bet you got him drunk at the Bad Boys Pub and then you loaded him into the car."

Adinolfi waved his Kalashnikov. "We didn't come here to listen to this bullshit," he shouted; he had a strong Roman accent.

"All right. We're listening," I replied amiably.

"You can take your proposal and stick it up your ass," the former mercenary went on, his tone combative. "You're in no position to dictate terms. If you want, we can duke it out, here and now. We're not afraid of you. Otherwise, get out of here and don't let us see you again."

I heaved a sigh. This was turning ugly, and I was right in the line of fire. My instinct was to drop to the floor and cover my head with both hands, expecting to hear a fusillade of gunshots. Instead, there was just one.

Bellomo, who'd taken care to remain behind his partner, had pulled out his gun and shot him in the back of the head. One shot, a sneak attack, and the Roman asshole, who hadn't realized he was the only one who could be sacrificed, dropped to the floor, dead on the spot.

His murderer threw the gun to the ground, followed by the submachine gun he was carrying over his shoulder. From one pocket of his combat vest he pulled a yellow envelope and tossed it to me. "That's twenty-six thousand euros," he explained, his voice quavering slightly. "That's all we can give you. Now or ever. We ask you to appreciate our goodwill."

I pretended to consult with my partners. They were probably lying to us about the money but the important thing was that someone had paid for Luigina Cantarutti's death.

We withdrew in silence, abandoning them to their fate, which wasn't really all that hard to imagine.

Ferdinando, the father, wouldn't be able to go on for long carrying the burden of the horror to which he'd become an accomplice. A heart attack, a stroke, or a fast-growing cancer was sure to free him from the armed robbery gone wrong that had defined his fate.

Lorenzo, paralyzed from the neck down, would have all the time in the world to cultivate his hatred, but he'd go on paying for it every minute of the rest of his life. He was, of all the pieces of shit in that story, the biggest loser, but I couldn't bring myself to feel any pity for him.

Ludovico "Vick" Bellomo. The traitor who hadn't hesitated to eliminate his partner was the filthiest of the bunch but, like all those of his kind, he was destined to survive. He'd make Adinolfi's corpse disappear, would spread the right lies, and then he'd become the owner of the Bad Boys Pub. Just waiting for the next friend to betray.

"Now it's Spezzafumo and the widow's turn," Beniamino commented.

I was sick and tired. "Let's take a couple of days off," I suggested. "After all, they're under control."

"I agree," said Rossini. "I can take advantage of the opportunity to take my friends back home."

"Are you sure you're not going to need them again?" asked Max.

"No," he replied. "I can handle those guys on my own."

I called the widow. "You can relax, we've settled things."

From the other end of the line, I heard a long sigh. "In a definitive manner, I trust."

"That's none of your business," I said, and hung up.

I was afraid to go to Pico's Club for fear I'd run into Cora's husband. So I waited for her at the usual café where she ate breakfast. She sat down beside me and smiled.

"I have the morning free," she said softly. "Do you have a place to take me that's not some seamy hotel room?"

My jazz woman really didn't like making love between the sheets. "Certainly," I replied. "I've been thinking about suggesting this place for a while now."

I made a phone call and took her to a recording studio midway between Mestre and Treviso. A nice place, and very advanced in terms of recording technology.

Cora looked like a little girl in a toy store. "Can I record?"

"There are no musicians," I said. "But you can make do with the basics."

She gave me a kiss and started talking intently with the sound technician. There was enough time to record just one piece, and she chose a song by Carmen Lundy, the musician she'd styled herself after, one of the singer's warhorses: *Old Friend*.

"I'm dedicating it to you," she told me before stepping into the soundproofed booth.

"I just hope you're not investing money in her," the technician muttered. "Technically she might be passable, but for an amateur, she's overreaching. There are passages where she's ridiculous."

I shrugged. "Everyone has their own version of jazz," I retorted, paraphrasing an old blues adage.

Two hours later Cora was holding a CD with her performance in her hands. She was happy. I dragged her into the musicians' break room. Just then it was deserted. I shut the door and turned the key and kissed her on the neck. She was humming to herself and she let me do what I wanted.

When we stretched out on a sofa, she said: "Slowly, nice and slow, kid."

No hurry, no urgency. Just slow tenderness, kisses, caresses. It was wonderful.

When we got back in the car she froze me to my seat with the three words I'd been afraid to hear from the beginning of our relationship. "I know everything."

I lit a cigarette and braced myself for the worst.

"All I had to do was ask my husband who told him about Pico's and he gave me your name. He told me a story about an unlicensed private investigator so stupid he didn't even notice I was screwing the piano player."

"The piano player?"

"Last night they had a fistfight. My spouse threw a tantrum and the piano player jumped him."

"He's in love with you."

"I figured as much."

She slipped the disc into the CD player and we listened to the song. It occurred to me that her choice had been intentional.

"You lied to me," Cora said bitterly. "I betrayed my husband. For a few moments of freedom from our lives, in order to make love without being weighed down by bad thoughts, we were forced to build castles of lies. I don't regret it but I don't know if I'll ever have the strength again to put on Cora's emerald-green dress."

"I don't want to be pathetic and try to justify myself, but I do have a few things to say."

"I don't want to hear them. I'm certain of your good intentions."

I sighed. This wasn't how it was supposed to end. We retreated into silence until I parked my car next to hers.

She caressed my cheek. "So long, kid."

I stopped in a well-stocked liquor store and bought a bottle of aged calvados. Back home, I shut myself in my room to listen to the blues, songs that told heartbreaking love stories, puzzling out the meaning of that farewell. Was it a "goodbye" or an "until we meet again"?

Before dinnertime I heard a knock on the door. "Will you condescend to join us?" Max the Memory shouted, furious. "The case isn't closed and you're behaving like a fucking high schooler."

I sat up on the bed and the room started spinning. "Coming," I slurred.

I went to the kitchen pantry and pulled out a bottle that contained a yellow liquid. A cleansing, herb-based solution that was particularly well suited for recovering from a bender. I gulped down a couple of mouthfuls and joined my friends.

Beniamino put his arm around my shoulder. "Did she leave you?"

"I'm not really sure," I replied. "But she found out I was lying to her."

"That's what always happens," Max commented.

"I had no other choice if I wanted to court her," I said in my own defense.

"Stories that start out complicated end up the same way," Rossini pronounced. Then he changed the subject. "Now let's have a nice plate of spaghetti and focus on Spezzafumo, okay?"

*

The following morning, after beating back a ferocious headache with a couple of Advils, I went to see Mario Bianchi.

"There are going to be a few extras on the tab," he pointed out, first thing, as he read through the reports. "We ended up having to tail the subjects."

"No problem."

"The three men went to the same place, once each, but at different times of day: a goldsmith's workshop in the Vicenza area," he continued, handing me a sheet of paper with all the information. "Our surveillance of the woman turned up nothing out of the ordinary."

I paid the bill and left. I'd been right; once they thought they were safe, the gang had gone straight back to work. Their cash reserves must have been down to their last few euros, which meant they needed to pull off a job. They'd had all the time they needed to carefully pick a target and the fact that they were checking it out with such care meant that it was just a few days until the robbery. They'd steal a car, don gloves and ski masks, and burst in armed and ready to shoot. The exact same approach that had led to Maicol Fecchio's agony and death.

The unwritten laws applied every bit as much to crimes that merely involved the use of weapons as they did to those that necessarily involved violence against their victims: home invasions and kidnappings were the acts of cowards and pariahs. Armed robberies are governed by one fundamental rule: the safety of those being robbed must be ensured. Going in with the assumption that a trigger was going to be pulled meant that it was a bad plan and should be abandoned.

Old Rossini considered armed robbery to be an art; he'd never shown up for his hits with a bullet chambered and he'd even been able to empty armored cars manned by armed guards without anyone getting hurt.

Personally, I had never liked armed robbery because weapons, generally speaking, scared me. But for all those years I'd lived off the armed robberies Beniamino had pulled, and I'd never allowed myself to say a thing about it.

"Assholes! Stupid assholes!" Rossini hissed in disbelief. "I don't want to have to go after those two overgrown kids, Denis and Giacomo, or whatever the fuck their names are. I made myself clear, very clear, but if they're going to ignore my warnings then words aren't going to be enough and mothers are going to be weeping over the graves of their sons."

"We can't afford to wipe out the whole gang," I put in. "The widow would try as hard as she could to make us pay the price, and we definitely don't want to find ourselves in a situation where we have to kill her, too."

"You have a better idea?" asked Beniamino.

"I don't know if it's a good one, but I think it's worth giving it a try: Tazio Bonetti."

"You're thinking about going to the fences?" Max asked, surprised.

"Yes."

"That's a risky move," the old gangster commented. "If negotiations don't turn out, then we'll be at war with them, too."

"We wouldn't do anything that reckless," I retorted, "and we'll settle for Spezzafumo. I'm inclined to think that, without their boss, these two enforcers are going to find some new line of business."

"You're an optimist," said Max. "But it's worth giving it a shot."

"If you don't mind, I'd like to go on my own this time," I declared.

My friends burst out laughing. "We were actually hoping you'd spare us another meeting with that nasty old geezer."

I pretended to be surprised. "Tazio isn't all that bad, for a fence."

I got in my car and headed toward Brescia, the interior of the Felicia vibrating with the sheer volume of the music. I was listening to Pork Chop Willie and doing my best to keep my mind off Cora. I was tempted to turn the car around and rush straight to her, but I knew I'd never do it. I had very different priorities at that moment and, in any case, getting a door slammed in my face was a very real risk. As well as the last thing I needed.

The heat was intolerable and for once I found myself complaining about my un-air-conditioned Škoda. I made it to Brescia around lunchtime and went straight to the fence's house. I hadn't warned him and he was sure to be extremely annoyed to have his lunch interrupted.

He lived in a villa surrounded by greenery in a residential neighborhood. The house was surrounded by a small, well-tended yard, but the windows on the ground floor were protected by metal bars and, on the second floor, by bulletproof glass. These days, even a major local crime boss was forced to take defensive measures against burglars.

His granddaughter opened the door. "We're eating lunch," she politely pointed out. "Couldn't you come back later? Maybe after my grandfather's had his nap?"

"I'm sorry, but I can't. Please tell him that it's Buratti and that this is an emergency."

I waited a couple of minutes and then I was ushered into a tiny sitting room which, to judge from the magazines scattered over the coffee table, must have been Bonetti's wife's favorite place in the house.

Tazio walked in, in sandals and a tank top. "Fuck, I was eating lunch," he complained.

"Sit down, Tazio," I said, cutting him off.

"You're in my house," he shot back, belligerently.

I came straight to the point. "If the widow Oddo and Spezzafumo were going to put their gang back together and plan a job, who would they turn to, to fence the gold?"

He froze for a couple of seconds, staring at me, then he went to shut the door. "Why are you bothering to ask? You already know the answer."

"I want to be straight with you," I said. "We ordered Spezzafumo and his two young partners in crime to retire from the business, and they chose to ignore us. Moreover, Nicola threatened us, and now the situation has been compromised. There's no avoiding a clash. Are you all sure you want to be involved?"

Bonetti tried to talk reason to me. "The plan dates back at least a year, but they never felt safe and they kept putting it off until now. They came to see me, I talked it over with the others, and now we're ready to unload the swag. There's a hell of a lot of money at stake. Can't you cut each others' throats afterwards?"

I ignored the question because it was likely to bring the conversation to an end. I pulled out a pack of cigarettes.

"There's no smoking in here," he informed me as he reached out for a heavy crystal ashtray that looked as if it hadn't been used for years.

I ignored that request as well. The fence had gotten on my nerves. "We'd like to save the lives of the two youngsters, Denis and Giacomo, but we can only do that if they stop pulling jobs."

"That's not our problem, Marco," he snapped out. "There are four of us involved in this deal, and rethinking the whole thing at this point is out of the question. I already know what the others would say. They'd invite you to wait and talk to them a week after the robbery."

"And if we turned down that invitation?"

"Then you'd force us to take sides with Spezzafumo," he replied. "But please don't paint us into that corner over a stupid matter of principle."

I took the last few puffs and crushed out the butt. "You're too strong for us," I pointed out. "You could easily field twenty armed men, and the only one on our side who pulls the trigger is Rossini."

The old fence's face lit up. "I see you're finally starting to listen to reason. All of us put together would be capable of wiping you off the map without breaking a sweat. But we're reasonable people and we're happy to give you carte blanche, after this deal is done."

I raised a hand to interrupt. He hadn't understood a thing. "If something unpleasant were to happen to yours truly or to Max the Memory, no one would think twice," I explained, "but if Rossini were to catch a bullet, his friends from across the border would come to avenge his death. Several French friends and a couple of Dalmatians, for sure. I just recently met the Dalmatians, they're professional killing machines. None of you would be left alive."

He laughed in my face. "You're bluffing."

"No. But you are, because you're the last guys who want to get caught up in a gang war. It would be bad for business. In this country, not even the various Mafias leave the streets littered with corpses anymore. Do you really want to be the ones to revive that old tradition—four broken-winded old fences? I'll say it again: Call off the deal."

He sighed. "It's too late, and let me repeat: This is the biggest job in the last ten years."

Spezzafumo's gang was about to swing into action. A matter of days, if not hours. Two days at the most. "Too bad for you," I said by way of farewell as I pulled open the door.

I went back to Padua and informed my friends.

"I've waited too long, if anything," said Rossini.

He procured a stolen motorcycle and, armed with a pair of revolvers, he went to the home of Nick the Goldsmith, in the countryside south of Padua, on the boundary with the province of Rovigo. He spoke to the young Polish woman who lived with Nick, and met the fair-haired child she held in her arms. The woman told Beniamino that Nicola would be away for another couple of days.

Beniamino asked her if that was Nicola's son and, with a broad smile, she told him he was. "He's my man and soon he's going to be my husband."

Our friend returned home with deep misgivings. "Who'll take care of them, after I've killed Spezzafumo?"

I saw my opening and I took it. "We can always reconsider how necessary this is."

"Do you want to have to watch your back for the rest of your life?" asked Max.

"He's not wrong," Rossini put in. "But right now all we can do is wait for events to unfold. Those three are hidden somewhere, waiting to carry out the robbery. In the end, that asshole Tazio Bonetti was right: We're going to have to settle our differences afterward."

"Siro Ballan," I blurted out suddenly. "I bet they're holed up at the luthier's place."

We looked at each other for a few seconds, savoring the idea of putting an end to the stalemate, but old Rossini reminded us: "That place is untouchable."

We moved to Punta Sabbioni, intending to stay there until we could come up with a better idea about what to do next.

We talked until we were blue in the face, trying to figure out a solution that would allow us to sidestep our own rules. On the one hand, old Rossini wouldn't budge about applying them; on the other, he hoped as much as anybody that he wouldn't be forced to go in guns blazing.

"I can't get the sight of Spezzafumo's kid out of my head," he kept saying in a worried voice.

It was an entirely workaday anonymous phone call to the armed robbery enforcement squad at Vicenza police headquarters that solved the case. When the Spezzafumo gang burst into the goldsmith's workshop, they found themselves surrounded by policemen ready to open fire. Nicola, Denis, and Giacomo put up their hands and wound up behind bars, facing the prospect of at least five or six years in—possibly even longer given the fact that they were armed with military-grade weapons.

According to a well-informed journalist, to whom I slipped three hundred euros, the tip had come in from a phone booth somewhere around Piove di Sacco. Which meant it had been the widow who betrayed her partners. The fences hadn't dirtied their hands and they'd killed the deal, negotiating with the only real boss. They must have told her that they were pulling out to avoid starting a war with old Rossini, and that the gang needed to be dissolved to prevent any future "misunderstandings." Those four bloodsuckers couldn't allow Gigliola to start working with other fences or they risked losing control of the market.

"Nothing personal, strictly business," Tazio most certainly had told her, stealing the line from some movie.

And the widow had been forced to make a hard choice: sell out her friends and give up on the idea of getting rich. She wasn't powerful enough to take on the fences, and she'd given in to their will.

No doubt they'd indemnified her in one way or another, probably by offering her a marginal role in the garment sector of their business. The thirty pieces of silver always get handed over, one way or another.

Our outlaw hearts couldn't conceive of betrayal. That was

totally alien to our worldview. But in the criminal underworld, everyone betrayed everyone else. It was the perfect solution, always ready to hand.

I waited for nightfall and drove over to Gigliola Pescarotto's house. I got out of the car and positioned myself in the middle of the street, my gaze fixed on the front of the house. I guessed that the sound of the car stopping in front of her villa would alarm her immediately, and I expected her to look out the window.

I saw a curtain move and a second later the woman's head appeared.

She gestured for me to phone her.

She looked at me for a couple of seconds and then withdrew slowly until she was swallowed up by darkness.

A few days later, news hit of a family tragedy. A father had shot and killed his paraplegic son and his wife and then turned his weapon on himself. And so, in the end, Ferdinando Patanè had worked up the nerve to take that pistol out of the drawer. According to the journalists, the motives for that deranged act could be traced back to the 2009 armed robbery, when young Lorenzo had been shot in the back by two still unidentified robbers, and to the ensuing tribulations endured by a family that had been abandoned by the state and found itself with no way out.

But the story was soon filed away. Just then, it served no one's interest. The most popular story was the "victory" of a town in the Treviso area that had succeeded in evicting a hundred or so immigrants who were being housed in a residential hotel. With equal parts ferocity and fear, the revolt against the "Africanization" of the region continued.

I went back to Pico's Club the last night before it closed for August. Cora wasn't there, that night the trio was playing, but, right up to the end, I held onto the hope that the jazz woman would saunter onstage for one last song.

I stayed there until daylight talking with the piano player about music and women, between swigs of alcohol and handfuls of peanuts, to keep from succumbing entirely to a weepy drunken bender.

"You know, I don't even know your name," I confessed when the time came to say goodbye. "I've known you by sight for years but we've never shaken hands."

"Duke Masini," he introduced himself. "My father loved jazz and dreamed that one day I'd become a musician. Probably a better one than I actually am, but you can't have everything."

I shut the place down and boarded my Felicia, heading for Pordenone. Blues from the stereo and warm air that came pouring in through the open windows.

The boy was waiting for me at the ground floor entrance to the apartment building, gripping the handle of a wheeled suitcase they'd bought from Chinese street vendors. His hair was neatly combed, the part straight—clearly the work of patient application with a wet comb. He wore a jacket that was too small for him and a pair of English-style shorts. He looked like a proper young man from times gone by who had stepped straight out of a yellowing photograph.

His uncle stood beside him, his arm wrapped around the boy's shoulder.

"Are you ready?" I asked him.

He bowed his head and mumbled words I couldn't understand. No, he was by no means ready for the journey he was about to undertake, but I was sure he'd soon change his mind. Or at least, that's what I hoped. My experience with human beings of that age was nonexistent, and with adults it had almost invariably proved useless.

He hugged his uncle, crying like a baby. It was a scene straight out of a nineteenth-century play where the villain of the week yanked the child away from his nearest and dearest to shut him up in a convent run by evil nuns.

"Take good care of him," the uncle stammered as he shook my hand.

He'd said the same words to me a few days earlier when we'd met at a lawyer's office. I'd insisted he bring his wife with him, a woman terrified by their precarious economic conditions and who eked out a living by gutting chickens at a local poultry farm. Even before the lawyer started laying out the reasons he'd asked them to come in, she'd tried every which way to excuse herself for being incapable of pretending to be Sergio's mother.

"I didn't bring him into the world," she said, getting worked up. "He's Luigina's baby. And she was such a strange girl: What if her son turns out like she did? And after all, it's not that I'm trying to be mean, but we really don't have the money, and we have two children of our own to raise."

I looked over at the lawyer in the hope that he'd stem that flood of words. His name was Eros Cocco, a good man in his early sixties, of Sardinian origins, who defended Roma and immigrants and therefore never earned a fucking cent. I'd turned to him because he was principled in his defense of civil rights and also because the money he'd make by safeguarding the interests of Luigina and her son would help prop up his financial situation a bit.

Cocco had suddenly reached out and grabbed both Signora Cantarutti's hands. "We understand your point of view perfectly, but now it's my turn to talk."

The lawyer had explained that he'd invited the husband and wife there today to inform them that there was news about Luigina and Sergio. Arnaldo, as her brother, would receive 100,000 euros' worth of indemnification.

The man was on the verge of fainting. "Where on earth does all that money come from?"

Cocco explained that this was a private donation, the result of a negotiation that had been handled by other lawyers.

Then he added that a trust fund had been set up to ensure that Sergio would be provided for and could afford tuition until he graduated from university. "But the condition is that your nephew be sent to live in a different family environment than yours. We haven't yet identified the family, but I will make arrangements at the earliest possible opportunity."

They'd accepted the terms with an exaggerated sense of gratitude, and this summer trip was part of the understanding.

They weren't bad people, but they certainly weren't up to the task of raising a boy like Sergio, a boy who would grow up marked by the fact that his father hadn't wanted him and that his mother had been a somewhat strange woman whom everyone had taken advantage of.

The money that the Patanès had managed to scrape together wouldn't be enough and Beniamino had sold Sylvie's jewelry and the house in Beirut to help those who were in need and had a right to it.

One afternoon he set out with a bag full of cash and went back to knock on Nicola Spezzafumo's front door. The Polish girl who had made the error of falling in love with an armed robber was on the verge of despair and old Rossini had given her a nice lump sum so she could take her little boy and go back to live with her parents and start a new life.

This too was a way to settle matters.

"Do you like the blues?" I asked Sergio when we got into the car.

"I don't know."

I slipped in one of Catfish's prescription CDs. The Altered Five Blues Band struck up *I'm in Deep*.

He listened for a few minutes, then started looking out the car window. I told him he was free to play the radio and he fooled around with the controls for a little while until he found a station that broadcast only Italian music. He knew lots of singers I'd never heard of. He explained that they came from reality shows. I had no difficulty taking him at his word. All Italy had turned into a reality show. I found out that he liked to talk and that, like all little kids, he loved stuffing himself with junk food. At a service area I gave him ten euros while I went to take a pee. When I got back, he'd already spent it all on potato chips and candy in unsettling colors.

He didn't ask any questions and I offered no explanations concerning the destination of that odd field trip. I was traveling in the company of a twelve-year-old boy and I was out of my comfort zone. He seemed so fragile; I was afraid I'd put my foot in it and hurt him somehow.

At last we reached Punta Sabbioni. Beniamino and Max were waiting for us on the deck of the *Sylvie*. Rossini was dressed like Peter O'Toole in *Lord Jim*.

Sergio was overcome with excitement and I had to help him climb aboard.

"On this pirate ship there are two rules that must be respected," Rossini started out in a voice that was deadly serious. "The first is that I'm the captain and everyone owes me unswerving obedience. The second is that when I make this gesture which means 'stitch your lips,'" he said, running his thumb and forefinger over his lips as if zipping them up, "everyone is required to keep whatever they've seen or heard to themselves. Agreed?"

"Yes."

They shook hands and Beniamino gave the order to cast off. Then he laid his hand on the boy's shoulder. "You want to see how to steer the best boat in the world?"

We sailed to the archipelago of the Kvarner islands and tied up on one of the least popular islands, where we'd rented a large villa overlooking the water.

That was how Sergio's summer began.

Under old Rossini's kind and careful tutelage, he learned to dive off the rocks into the salt water, to get up in the middle of the night to set sail in a fishing trawler, to throw the first punch so that other boys wouldn't be able to bully him.

Max introduced him into the world of adventure books, the Internet, and the movies.

He fell asleep in the arms of old whores and working smugglers. He was adorable, curious, and kind, and everyone loved him.

Every so often he and Beniamino would go off on their own and Sergio would tell the old bandit about his mother, about what had happened to her. Most of all he wanted to understand why Luigina had always been considered so different. The old bandit would take him on his knee and wrap his arms around him and teach him how to defend himself against the cruel world of grown-ups.

I remained at a distance and watched. I never knew how to be spontaneous with Sergio; every word I said, every thing I did was always the product of complicated thought processes. Remaining on the margins allowed me to understand that this wasn't just his summer. It was also ours. After many years, we were finally able to enjoy an interval of relative peace and quiet.

One night, a Danish girl came in on the last ferry. Blonde, with skin the color of milk. The currents of her life had pushed her all the way to our little island. She understood that she had fetched up among other shipwrecked souls and decided to come live with us; she settled into an unoccupied room, spoke very little, but seemed to like our company. She was attractive and I thought about trying to strike something up with her, but for the first time a woman seemed too young and I decided to let it drop.

Sergio was very curious about the "foreign woman," as Max had dubbed her. He was the only one who seemed able to draw her out of the lethargy that afflicted her, speaking to her in his junior-high English.

She'd claimed her name was Bente but Rossini, who had searched her room to make sure she didn't represent a threat to the boy, said that there was a different name on her "Swedish" passport. And that she didn't have a penny to her name.

We didn't give a damn about these little white lies. She lied because she couldn't possibly know that she could trust us; that there was no secret more terrible than the ones we were already keeping in our hearts and in our memories.

We found a way to give her a little money without offending her. She barely thanked us, as if it hardly mattered to her.

When the time came to leave the island she asked if she could stay in the villa a little longer. We paid another month's rent and the landlady promised she'd keep an eye out for her.

We returned to Punta Sabbioni the first week of September; a few days later Sergio was scheduled to start school again. We found the lawyer, Cocco, waiting for us. In the meantime, he'd found a young couple in Trieste who were interested in taking Sergio in, and eventually adopting him. A ridiculously long, complicated, and difficult process in our country, but the lawyer had high hopes.

I watched Sergio as he sobbed brokenhearted in the arms of Beniamino and Max. He'd understood it was unlikely he'd ever see any of us again. We'd always been straight with him on that point. He was greatly changed. His hair was sun-bleached, his eyebrows were white as tow, and his skin was the color of leather. He'd grown.

At last he left. Loaded down with gifts and memories of the strangest summer of his life.

And my friends left, too. Just enough time to fill the speedboat's tanks and they were gone. Old Rossini had some business to tend to and the fat man had decided to accompany him.

I remained on land. I missed my jazz woman. But when I got back to Padua I discovered that Pico's had been shuttered for good. A construction crew was already at work turning it into the branch office of some unfamiliar bank. I felt sadness at the sight of the old sign lying in the rubble.

For several mornings, I staked out Cora's apartment building. At last I saw her leave. I immediately understood that she had gone back to being Marilena. I simply made my presence known. She looked at me, perhaps she even gave me a slight smile, but she didn't stop. She kept on walking, straight to her car, started it up, and disappeared around a curve in the road.

I smoked a cigarette but couldn't thread together anything resembling a complete thought. I felt shattered, as if I'd gone to pieces once and for all, even though I'd always known that my relationship with her was all but bound to end the way it had.

Just then, I was unemployed and I didn't know what to do with myself. I didn't even feel like getting drunk.

I phoned Antonio Santirocco, the mayor of the blues.

"I need a gig," I told him.

And so I went back to working with the Triade. Bob on keyboards, Babe on guitar, Antonio on drums, and Stefano, the actor who told tales of blues and criminals.

We traveled every day, and every night we played a different club. And then we wound up in a hotel room with dirty windows, though it hardly mattered: There was never anything interesting to see.

I was living from day to day without much effort, limiting myself to keeping a safe distance from everything, not expecting anything, but not feeling too sorry for myself anymore, either. I met a couple of interesting women. Delia and Giannina. For Giannina in particular it would have been worth quitting the tour and saying farewell to my musician friends, but I kept myself from doing it. For her own good. I didn't want to do her the dirty trick of vanishing into thin air when I got a certain phone call. Because that's exactly what would have happened.

I kept on keeping on while waiting for another case where we'd need to step in to help straighten things out. The solution was almost never as simple as determining the truth. We needed to protect our clients' interests and, as much as possible, put things right, while respecting the rules of free men with outlaw hearts.

EPILOGUE

The fact that life was strange and capable of springing surprises on you when you least expect them was something I'd long known, but I could never have imagined the phone call I got; it was from the last person I expected. It was a lazy late afternoon, and I was sitting at a table at a bar on the piazza of a charming little village in Romagna drinking a beer. My friends from the Triade, the all-Italian organ trio led by the "mayor of the blues" Antonio Santirocco, were shut up in a club doing rehearsals for that evening's concert. My cell phone starting ringing and I waited until the fourth ring, just for effect.

"This is Giorgio Pellegrini. Don't hang up."

The surprise left me speechless. The last time I'd seen him, I'd begged old Rossini to shoot him. Beniamino had refused because we'd promised him immunity to save the life of a kidnap victim. Giorgio Pellegrini was the worst criminal I'd ever met. Murderer, traitor, blackmailer, pimp, rapist. The list of his crimes was long. Too long to allow him to go on living, but he'd proven to be damned cunning, always able to dig himself a bolt-hole of some kind.

The way he'd done with us. He'd fled Padua, pursued by a warrant for his arrest issued by the district attorney and by a promise from Rossini that the next time we met he'd be a dead man.

"What do you want?" I asked.

"I didn't do it."

"Do what?"

I heard him sigh. "So you don't know anything?"

I hadn't read a paper or listened to the news in days. "I don't know fuck all," I blurted out in irritation.

"Martina and Gemma were murdered."

His wife and his lover. I knew them well. Two fully consensual victims of Pellegrini's perversions. They'd been dismayed at having been abandoned, but as far as I knew they'd begun running La Nena, the restaurant that handsome Giorgio had made famous all over the region.

"I want to hire you guys," he said. "I want you and your partners to find out who killed them."

"You've called the wrong person. The only thing I'd be willing to do for you is witness your death."

"But first you and that museum piece of a friend of yours would have to find me. In the meantime, you can look into the case. You're mercenaries, you work on contract. I don't see where the problem is."

"The problem is you, Pellegrini."

"Don't be stupid," he retorted, all smarm. "Otherwise you're running the risk of doing it for free because I'm sure that when all is said and done, you're not going to be able to resist the temptation to stick your noses into it anyway. I know you're going to want to find out the truth behind the brutal murder of two poor, innocent girls."

The son of a bitch. I'd forgotten about his uncanny ability to understand people. I changed the subject. "You don't really give a damn about them, do you?" I accused him.

"Sincerely, not all that much," he explained, still speaking in that pesky tone. "I'm interested in figuring out who's behind it, who's trying to flush me out by murdering my 'nearest and dearest.'"

"The list of your victims is long enough to fill a local phone book," I objected. "Just try to imagine how many people go to sleep every night with dreams of taking revenge on you."

"Revenge has nothing to do with it. The motive for the killings is definitely something else," he retorted confidently.

"Tell the cops about it," I suggested. "They're sure to listen to you, since you're one of their confidential informants."

"I used to be. Then we lost touch, the cops and me," he huffed. "Right now, the police are stumbling around in complete darkness. When the district attorney decides it's time to get some results, they'll accuse me of the crime and wrap up the case in the space of a week."

"Nothing could be simpler."

"But you're not going to settle for the official version."

"Don't kid yourself."

He snickered. "I know you, Buratti, I've seen you at work. You're obsessed with the truth, you're not going to give up a chance to work on this case. I could arrange to advance you fifty thousand euros in a matter of days. The rest when the job is completed."

"I told you: No!"

"Then you're going to investigate free of charge. Offering you money was just a nice way of salving your conscience of the grim thought that you'll be working for a shady character like yours truly."

Pellegrini hung up and I finished drinking my beer; my hand was trembling slightly. You couldn't trust that character even when he was telling the truth. He always had a plan, every single move he made was thought out well in advance. And that phone call was no exception.

I held out long enough to drink another beer, and then I rushed out in search of an Internet café so I could dig up some information about the double murder.

When I saw their photographs, I felt sorry for those two poor women. Martina and Gemma had always paid dearly for the joke destiny had chosen to play on them by delivering them into the hands of Giorgio Pellegrini. He'd manipulated them so thoroughly that they had no will of their own. They'd become docile marionettes, and they'd remained loyal to him even after he vanished from their lives.

According to the investigators, they'd been surprised by one or more people inside the restaurant just before closing time, when the cooks and the waiters had already left. They'd been forced down into the basement and there they'd been tied up, tortured, and then strangled with piano wire.

The day's take had been found in Gemma's purse, ready to be deposited at the bank.

Once robbery was ruled out as a motive, the police shifted their focus to Giorgio Pellegrini's shadowy past, looked for a motive there. He was currently wanted and on the run.

Nonsense. Too ridiculous to be anything other than a red herring. The investigators had done their best to keep the journalists at bay: At last the press had caught hold of a case they could cover for a good long time to come. In exchange, they'd been tossed a few succulent bones to gnaw on, but the cops and judges had treated Pellegrini with exaggerated care, almost as if they were eager to protect him, forcing the press to fan out in pursuit of leads they knew would play well, but which were devoid of any real investigative basis: gangs from eastern Europe, immigrants who, back home, were professional bandits, serial killers, satanic sects, and other bullshit.

Certainly this had been the work of professionals. At least three. One outside the restaurant, acting as a lookout. And two inside. The fact that piano wire had been used to finish off the two women was a message meant for Giorgio Pellegrini. It said: We're good at what we do; efficient, dangerous, and lethal.

If what he said was true and the motive wasn't revenge, then this was the work of a criminal organization powerful enough to have its own well-trained, professional killers. I found myself examining the case as if I really had been hired to investigate, and I had to make a real effort to focus on anything else.

Pellegrini had used the right arguments to capture my interest, but I had no intention of giving in. You simply can't work for a client you'd like to see dead with all your heart. It's neither right nor healthy.

I spent the evening with Triade's purebred blues, but every once in a while, memories of my interactions with Martina and Gemma bubbled dangerously to the surface, and I was forced to thrust them back into a corner of my mind with a healthy shot of calvados.

At six in the morning, the cops entered my room using a skeleton key. They could just as easily have come in two hours later and we all would have gotten more sleep, but there are certain habits that law enforcement isn't about to break.

I opened my eyes and saw Inspector Campagna, who was, for the occasion, wearing a white and light-blue Hawaiian shirt, sitting on the edge of my bed waving a pair of handcuffs.

"I've never understood people who go to a restaurant and then complain to the staff because the portions are too large," he began while his colleagues started turning the room upside down. "Why don't they just mind their own fucking business? They complain so much that they talk the proprietors into making portions smaller, and then we're all worse off. If there's too much pasta, think of your health and leave it on the plate. Don't you think so, Buratti?"

"You come all the way down here with your boyfriends to discuss this bullshit?" I asked, my mouth fuzzy with sleep.

"And to take you back to Padua where the pleasure of your presence is requested at police headquarters for a nice little chat."

"What's going on, Campagna?" I asked, a little worried now.

"Nothing," he replied as he handed me my trousers. "It's just that you still don't know how to behave at the table and now we're going to give you a slap on the wrist."

Padua. Interrogation room at police headquarters.

It was lunchtime, and no one had shown up yet. They'd locked me up in the usual cubbyhole that reeked of sweat, coffee, and stale cigarette smoke, in defiance of Italian law. Of course they'd confiscated my cigarettes.

I was pretty sure they were watching me through the usual two-way mirror. They wanted to make me think I was in real trouble, the kind of trouble that lands you first in court and then in prison for a certain number of years. Maybe it was even true. Maybe Gigliola Pescarotto, the widow Oddo, had decided to rat me out, or else the idea had come to Nicola Spezzafumo. The only thing I had to do was wait to find out just what was happening.

I managed to maintain the calm required for the situation only because I'd been through this kind of thing before, and I knew the world of law enforcement down to the last detail. Deep down, though, I was scared to death. Scared of going to prison.

After another couple of hours, the monotony of which had been interrupted only by a shouting match with the guards standing sentinel to get them to take me to the bathroom, a babe who might have been a cover girl showed up, accompanied by Campagna.

She was blonde, with a ponytail, perfect features, long legs, and tits and an ass that looked as if they'd been drawn by a master illustrator. She sat down across the table from me, smoothed down the hem of her designer skirt suit, and looked me up and down with an assertive air.

Then she gestured to Campagna, who hastened to turn on a small tape recorder. It must have been a very good brand, because you could hear both my voice and Pellegrini's perfectly.

I heaved a sigh of relief. The situation I was in wasn't all that serious after all.

"Giorgio Pellegrini has started using the SIM card of the cell phone that he had when he was still in Padua," the official explained. "That's why we were able to record the phone call."

The bastard had to have known that the investigators would be ready to listen. I wondered why he'd chosen to bring them into the middle of all this. Maybe so he could inform them of his innocence. Or else, no, that son of a bitch had decided to frame me and hand me over to the cops. Distracted by my complex reasoning, I missed the beginning of what the good-looking female cop was telling me and interrupted her very politely, asking if she could start over again from the beginning.

"Are you dimwitted? Stupid? Do you suffer from some kind of mental pathology? Or did your mother give you syphilis during pregnancy?" the woman asked, speaking in machine gun bursts in a strong Milanese accent. "Do you think we had you brought so we could chat? Or do you just think that we don't deserve your attention?"

Any thoughts of kindness suggested by her attractive appearance vanished at that moment. "With whom do I have the pleasure of speaking?" I asked.

She pointed to her underling. "With Inspector Giulio Campagna," she replied, her voice flat.

"What's that mean?"

"Haven't you figured that out by now?"

I, too, knew that game. The only way to defend yourself was to interrupt the stream of questions, because you'd never get an answer. Just more questions.

The official waited for me to respond, then went straight to the point. "We want you to accept Pellegrini's offer and

184 · MASSIMO CARLOTTO

investigate the murders. With your friends, of course. We won't interfere."

I would have liked to know whom she meant with that "we." And, after all, it was pretty clear that it was going to end badly for everyone, and not just for Pellegrini. There wasn't a single good reason to offer her our heads on a silver platter. We'd have done their dirty work for them and all we'd get in exchange would be a cell with a view of the yard in a maximum-security prison. That is, unless the whole deal was so filthy that the only thing to do was clean house, top to bottom, an operation that would involve executions and shallow graves.

"No," I said, addressing Campagna.

"No?" the policewoman echoed, raising her voice and jumping to her feet. "Listen good, you miserable piece of shit," she hissed. "Unless you do exactly as I say, your friends are going to wind up in prison. We know where they are and the minute they touch land we'll search the *Sylvie* and find just enough kilos of heroin and cocaine to bring down a minimum sentence of fifteen years. Rossini's a tough character and he can do the time, even if he'll go straight into a hospice when he's released, but Max, with his health problems, won't survive more than four years, five, tops."

She reached out her hand and Campagna gave her a file, which she slapped under my nose. It was Max's hospital chart. It looked like the original.

"We've had it examined by one of our experts," the policewoman went on. "What I tell you is the truth and I can assure you that we'll make it our business to ensure that every day behind bars will be a 'special' one for him."

Maybe she was bluffing. Or maybe she wasn't. I was too confused to figure that out. I tested the ground by, again, refusing outright.

"The little turd has a pair of balls on him," the woman commented, feigning admiration. She leveled her forefinger at

me, straight and long as a gun barrel. "Meanwhile, you'll be
out, free and at large. We'll circulate a rumor that you were the
one who sold out your friends, and that you're now a police
informant."

"No one's going to fall for that," I shot back ferociously.

Campagna walked over and leaned close, placing a hand on
my shoulder. "She's not like normal human beings," he said,
referring to his superior officer. "She comes from another
planet where playing dirty is the rule. She'll screw you unless
you do what she says."

"She'll screw us whatever we do," I thought to myself.

The woman burst into a forced laugh. "Campagna, you're
as pathetic as those shirts of yours. I'm going to ask the chief
of police why on earth he lets you wear them. Now get out of
this room."

The inspector obeyed, paying no heed to the insult.

The official sat down again. "All right then, Buratti, what's
your decision?"

"It seems to me I have no choice."

The lady cop gave me a long, hard, derisive look. "You're
all the same," she commented; then she ordered me to send a
text to Pellegrini, accepting the case and the money.

"Exactly what do you want from us?" I asked in a low
voice.

"I want you to stay out in plain view."

I pretended I hadn't understood. "Explain yourself."

"I want you to investigate. Or at least pretend to. We don't
care which," she explained in a bored voice. "The important
thing is that you give the impression you're searching for whoever committed that double murder, and that Pellegrini fall for
it sufficiently that he stays in touch."

"You don't need us to arrest him."

"True enough. But we have other priorities."

"And we're the pawns who can be sacrificed."

"I'm glad to see you understand. For that matter, you have quite the bill to pay. I don't know how on earth you've managed to stay out of jail these past few years, but the time has come to put an end to your fucking shenanigans."

The policewoman's flat sincerity made my blood run cold. "You don't have any evidence against us. Not even a hint of a lead, otherwise you wouldn't be playing dirty tricks like planting drugs aboard the *Sylvie*."

"We've collected a series of rumors that could turn into the pages of a deposition any day now."

"Horseshit."

She shook her head. The ponytail brushed her shoulders. "I'm sorry to give you more bad news, but Giorgio Pellegrini told me all about the Swiss woman and your activity as unlicensed investigators. A nice little story worth three life sentences without parole. One apiece."

Suddenly it dawned on me. That piece of shit was once again angling for judicial immunity so he could go back to playing the model citizen, and he'd made himself available to the cops. As a show of good faith he'd told them, in his own way of course, the "truth" about the events that had forced him to run from the law. But that would never have been enough to keep him out of jail. Pellegrini must have offered them a much tastier dish—probably that he'd been operating as an undercover agent, and that something had gone horribly wrong, and that it had cost Martina and Gemma their skins.

I looked the woman in the eye. I was certain that the idea of dragging us into it had been hers. Pellegrini had sold us down the river and she had come to the conclusion that we might turn out to be useful.

"Pellegrini lies as easily as he breathes," I said. "He's fed you a line without giving you any evidence."

"We don't need any," the policewoman reminded me. "And

in any case, Giorgio is so convincing that it's a pleasure just to listen to him."

She pulled my cigarettes and lighter out of my jacket pocket. "Smoke, Buratti. I know it's what you need more than anything else right now. Then you'll leave and get something strong to drink. Calvados, of course, which you'll savor while listening to that negro music."

That contemptuous display of details about my private life managed to drag a smile out of me. The conceited police-woman had read our files and listened to secondhand gossip, but hadn't the slightest idea who we really were. She judged us according to parameters straight out of the police academy, things that didn't apply to us. Our outlaw hearts noticed the difference, rendered the abyss that separated us impossible to bridge.

Now an official from who knew which division of the intel-ligence services was convinced she had me by the balls, taking it for granted that I'd talk my friends into stooping so low as to work for them, to march toward the enemy fire like so many puppets on strings. She had no idea how wrong she was. We had no generals, no masters dominating our lives.

"It strikes me as unnecessary to point out that we'll keep you on a long leash, but don't try to take advantage," the policewoman added from the door. "We're fast at picking up runaway shitheads."

Island of Prvić, Dalmatia.

The tourists had already left for the season and the bay where we'd dropped the *Sylvie*'s anchor was dark and silent. The water was chilly and still.

I'd reached my friends, hightailing it out of Padua the exact moment they let me go. I'd picked up an emergency cell phone and alerted them.

We'd arranged to meet in the port city of Šibenik, which I'd reached by train and bus. That's where Beniamino and Max had picked me up.

I wasn't on the run. The policewoman's words were to be considered with the utmost seriousness. It was just that we needed a little time to talk and make some decisions that were of fundamental importance to our future.

The situation was deadly serious. The minute I came on board I apologized to my friends for having been careless enough to entertain a conversation with Pellegrini.

"You couldn't have guessed it would turn out to be a booby trap," said Max.

The salt air had done him good and he'd lost a few pounds. His face was baked by the sun and his long hair hung down his neck. Rossini, too, was looking well. His smuggling operation was back up and running, moving goods and people across the Adriatic, and the fat man had been keeping him company.

"It was going to happen sooner or later," had been his only comment, as he uncorked a bottle of Istrian Malvasia.

We indulged in a lavish dinner before settling down to deal with harsh reality. A long and exhausting discussion during which I was forced to repeat over and over every last word uttered over the phone and at police headquarters.

A little before dawn, in the parlor of the *Sylvie*, silence fell as Max set about making the first espresso of the new day.

"There's only one sure thing about this situation, and that's that once again Giorgio Pellegrini is the linchpin of some obscure criminal operation," he reflected as he filled the demitasse cups.

"And his death would have the benefit of clearing the table," old Rossini put in. "All we should do now is find him, kill him, and then settle matters with that bitch from the intelligence agency."

"And the same for Martina and Gemma's murderers," I concluded.

Neither of my friends objected. The plan was drawn up or

at least sketched out, and there was nothing more to add. Max turned on the radio and tuned it to a station that was broadcasting the six o'clock news. Beniamino switched on the winch and hoisted the anchor.

I went on deck and sat on a chair in the stern to enjoy the view of the sea, the sky, and the island. After days of tension I finally felt tranquil. I didn't have the faintest idea how things were going to turn out, but I'd share my friends' fate and we'd hold our heads high. I couldn't hope for better.

ABOUT THE AUTHOR

Massimo Carlotto was born in Padua, Italy. In addition to the many titles in his extremely popular "Alligator" series, he is also the author of *The Fugitive, Death's Dark Abyss, Poisonville, Bandit Love,* and *At the End of a Dull Day.* One of Italy's most popular authors and a major exponent of the Mediterranean Noir novel, Carlotto has been compared with many of the most important American hardboiled crime writers.